April came skidding down the slope. "Michael!" she screamed. "Artie! Wait a minute. Please wait!" Breathless, she reached them.

"Forget it, April," Michael said without looking at her. "There's nothing you can say that will make me change my mind."

April grabbed hold of Artie. "Please, Artie. Can't you see what a stupid idea this is?"

Artie pulled down his visor. "I've got my pride, too, April. I can't back out now."

"Whenever you're ready," Michael called.

"On your mark," called Artie.

"Get set," yelled Michael. The engines of their bikes roared to life.

April was frozen as she watched Michael and Artie fly over the rough terrain. They were almost even from the start. Then, as they reached the steep incline, Michael swerved suddenly. As Michael pulled to the right, he cut directly into Artie's path. Artie turned sharply to avoid a crash.

April screamed as Artie's bike went out of control and he pitched over the bars, somersaulting through the air like a rag doll. It was something out of her worst nightmare. Immediately she started running down the slope. "Please let him be all right," she whispered, stumbling over the rocky incline. "Please, please, please . . ."

THE GIRL THEY BOTH LOVED

Written by
Kate William

Created by
FRANCINE PASCAL

BANTAM BOOKS
NEW YORK · TORONTO · LONDON · SYDNEY · AUCKLAND

RL 6, IL age 12 and up

THE GIRL THEY BOTH LOVED
A Bantam Book / November 1991

Sweet Valley High is a registered trademark of Francine Pascal

Conceived by Francine Pascal

Produced by Daniel Weiss Associates, Inc.
33 West 17th Street
New York, NY 10011

Cover art by James Mathewuse

ISBN 0-553-29226-9

Published simultaneously in the United States and Canada

Bantam Books are published by Bantam Books, a division of Bantam Doubleday Dell Publishing Group, Inc. Its trademark, consisting of the words "Bantam Books" and the portrayal of a rooster, is Registered in U.S. Patent and Trademark Office and in other countries. Marca Registrada. Bantam Books, 666 Fifth Avenue, New York, New York 10103.

PRINTED IN THE UNITED STATES OF AMERICA

OPM   0 9 8 7 6 5 4 3 2

THE GIRL THEY
BOTH LOVED

One

"Almost there," Michael Harris said as he drove his Trans-Am past the Sweet Valley Civic Center on his way to school.

"Oh, no," groaned April Dawson. "Not already!" She pulled her compact out of her bag and immediately began to check her makeup.

Every weekday morning Michael drove April to school. Every weekday morning when they passed the Civic Center Michael announced, "Almost there," and April said, "Not already!" and hurriedly took out her mirror.

Michael started to laugh. "Who'd believe that one of the best dirt bikers in Sweet Valley wears lipstick?"

April turned to him with a grin. With her thick dark hair and big brown eyes she did look more like a cheerleader than a dirt biker. "I

1

have to wear lipstick to make up for the fact that I have no fingernails left and my hair is squashed by a helmet most of the time," she said, laughing.

They stopped at an intersection. "You're still the prettiest girl in Sweet Valley as far as I'm concerned," he said softly, "squashed hair or not."

"Does that mean that you'll go to the movies with me tomorrow night?" April asked. April was a junior at Sweet Valley High and Michael was a senior. They had been going together for a while, but she still found it difficult to get him to do anything with her that didn't involve a dirt bike. If Michael wasn't riding his bike, he was working on it. And if he wasn't riding it or working on it, he was thinking about it. The next night the Plaza Theatre was beginning a series of films by Alfred Hitchcock, and she was hoping she could convince Michael to come along.

"Movie?" Michael repeated. "Tomorrow night?"

April sighed. "Yes, Michael. A movie. I told you about the film festival. It starts tomorrow night and I'd really like to go."

Michael peered anxiously at the passing traffic. "But tomorrow's Friday," he informed her.

"Exactly," she said, trying not to sound too exasperated. "Michael, this may come as a surprise to you, but a lot of couples go to the movies on Friday nights. *Together*."

2

"April," he said, obviously not listening, "am I OK on the right?"

A cautious driver herself, April dutifully checked the right again. "Yes," she said a little snappishly, "you're clear."

April drummed on the door as they pulled into traffic. As much as she liked Michael, it often seemed to her that she was always the one who made compromises in their relationship. If Michael wanted to spend the weekend tuning his engine, she sat and watched. If Michael wanted to spend the weekend testing out a new course, she was right behind him on her bike. But if *she* wanted to do something—like go to a film festival—she either did it alone or didn't go at all. April took a deep breath. She had made up her mind. She wasn't going to let the matter drop without a struggle. Not this time.

"So," she persisted, "will you come with me or not?"

Michael shook his head. "You know I'd love to go with you, but we have an important rally on Saturday. I really think we should both get a good night's sleep so we're ready for it."

April pretended to bang her head against the door frame. She should have known he would say something like that! Michael probably wouldn't go to the hottest party ever given in southern California if it was the night before a meet. She fought back a smile. Never mind going to a party, she thought; Michael wouldn't go to his own graduation if it was on the day of a meet. The truth was that dirt bike racing was the most important thing in the world to him. He took it very seriously. But though Michael lived for dirt biking, April didn't. They had teamed up when they first met, and started entering relay races. Over the months, they had established a solid reputation for themselves. But April had a lot of other interests that were important to her, too.

"Please, Michael," April pleaded. "I'd be a lot more ready for the rally if we did something I really enjoyed the night before."

The car came to a stop and Michael turned off the engine. Then, almost as though she hadn't spoken, he said, "We might even think about getting to the course a little early on Saturday, just to check it out again. Let's not forget all that rain we had yesterday."

"Michael," April said, "it's not like this is a major competition or anything. It's just a warm-up rally."

Michael opened his door. "It's major as far as I'm concerned. Artie Western's going to be riding."

April opened her door. Artie Western! If April had a dollar for every time she had heard Michael say that name, she would be as rich as Lila Fowler. Ever since she had met Michael, every other sentence out of his mouth seemed to be about Artie Western. *Artie Western gets all*

Western isn't half as good a rider
Iestern, I'll show him.

run to catch up with Michael,
ly striding ahead of her toward
ig deal!" she called after him.
always rides, and you usually

ped so abruptly that she almost
im. "I don't usually beat him,"
he corrected her, turning around. "We usually
come in about even."

"OK," April sighed, "so you usually come in
about even. What's the difference, Michael? It's
the sport that I love, not whether we win or
lose."

He started walking again. "Well, not me. I
ride to win, not to have a good time. And as
for Artie Western . . ."

His voice sounded so serious that April turned
to him in surprise. "Michael—" she began.

But he cut her off. "I'd rather give up riding
forever than have to admit that Artie Western's
better than I am."

April stared at him. She knew that Michael
and Artie had been best friends until about a
year before. Not only that, but they'd ridden
together and had been considered the team to
beat. But why they were no longer friends, and
why Michael had such a chip on his shoulder
when it came to Artie, she didn't know, because Michael refused to tell her.

"But why?" she demanded. "Why do you feel like that?"

"I don't want to talk about it," Michael mumbled, striding across the lawn. "You wouldn't understand."

April stayed where she was, hugging her books to her chest. "It doesn't look like we'll ever find out if I'd understand or not," she said to his vanishing back. "Because you won't give me the chance."

April usually ate her lunch with Michael, but that day she decided she could use a little break from his company. As she walked into the cafeteria she spotted Jessica Wakefield, Maria Santelli, Amy Sutton, and Lila Fowler sitting together. Although she was not really in their group, they had been very friendly to her lately. Lila and Jessica had even asked her to go shopping with them the week before. April decided to join them.

Maria smiled at her as she pulled out a chair, but no one else paid much attention. They were all listening to Jessica.

"I just don't know if I can stand one more minute of Sweet Valley," Jessica was saying loudly as April sat down. Jessica shook her head and rolled her blue-green eyes. She looked around the table at her friends with an anguished expression on her pretty face.

Her friends just stared at her. They knew from experience that Jessica was almost always

6

either extremely excited about something, or looking for something to be extremely excited about.

"I mean, really," Jessica continued, "the weather's awful."

"Awful? In southern California?" Maria smiled and pointed toward the cafeteria windows. "Jessica, it's absolutely beautiful outside."

"But yesterday it poured." Jessica lifted the top of her sandwich and peered at it suspiciously. "It poured, and my hair went as straight as a ruler." She dropped her sandwich back onto the table. "What I need is to be somewhere interesting. Somewhere sophisticated and exciting." She sighed dramatically. "Somewhere where things happen."

Lila smiled wistfully. "It's a shame you can't afford to go to Rome," she said to Jessica. "There are the most fabulous shops there." As the daughter of one of the wealthiest men in Sweet Valley, Lila had traveled more than any of her friends, and didn't mind letting them know that whenever she could.

Jessica shot her a look. "I'm not talking about shopping in Europe," she snapped. "I'm talking about feeling that my life is empty and meaningless."

Amy started to laugh. "You're talking about the fact that there hasn't been a big party for a couple of weeks."

Lila grinned. "I think it's just that Jessica's run out of boys to date."

7

Jessica turned to April. "See what I mean?" she asked. "They don't realize that there are more profound things in life than going out with boys."

"That's not what you said when you were planning to go to Hawaii to meet the boy of your dreams," Lila reminded her.

Recently Jessica had been convinced that she'd found the love of her life in a dream she kept having. The dream had taken place in Hawaii. Jessica had been determined to meet her dream lover, even if it meant swimming all the way there. "That was different," Jessica said quickly. "He wasn't just any boy. He was special."

"Yeah," put in Amy. "Because he didn't exist."

April held up her hands. "Don't talk to me about boys," she said with a laugh. "I'm beginning to think that I'll never understand them."

"You're not supposed to," Lila said, delicately wiping her mouth on a paper napkin. "That's what makes them so fascinating."

Maria touched April's shoulder. "I know what you mean," she said with a sympathetic smile. "There are times when you'd think we came from different planets."

April looked at Maria in surprise. Maria was dating Winston Egbert now, but she had once been engaged to Michael Harris. *Which of them is Maria talking about?* April wondered. She took a sip of juice and decided to change the subject. "It sounds to me like you're a little bored," she said to Jessica. "Why don't you come to the dirt bike rally on Saturday? Mike and I are entered in the relay."

"Dirt bike rally?" Jessica asked doubtfully.

April nodded enthusiastically. "You should come, Jess. It's really a lot of fun."

"Wait a minute," Lila interrupted. She pointed a granola bar at April. "Are you telling us that *you* actually race?"

April nodded. "I've been doing it for three years now. My big brother got me into it when I was still in middle school." April blushed. "That's how I got to know Mike," she explained. "At the track."

"Love at first bike," Jessica teased, but she looked a little intrigued. "I don't really know much about dirt bike racing except that it involves dirt and bikes," she admitted. A mischievous grin lit up her face. "But there must be some cute boys there." Jessica tilted her head. "Maybe I *will* come. At least it would be a change."

April was thinking about Michael as she walked to her last class. She had fallen for him from almost the first moment she noticed him at a rally. He had just won the advanced 125 moto, and was bent over beside his bike, adjusting his boot. He had looked up and caught her watching him, and he had smiled. She'd smiled back. When they first started dating, she had felt incredibly lucky. Not only did she and Michael share a common interest, but he was intelligent, good-looking, and fun to be with. As time went on, though, he seemed to become more involved in racing and less involved with her. As long as they were talking about bikes or racing everything was terrific, but if the subject turned to something more personal, he shut her out.

April was so involved in her thoughts, she walked right into Maria Santelli and Elizabeth Wakefield. "Oh, I'm so sorry," April said, stooping down to help them pick up the books they had dropped. "I don't know where I was. I didn't even see you."

Maria laughed good-naturedly. "Maybe *you* were on another planet. Have you figured them out yet?"

April grinned. "You mean boys?"

Maria turned to Elizabeth. "April was saying at lunch that she didn't think she'd ever understand boys."

Elizabeth smiled. It was the same smile that brightened the face of her twin sister, Jessica. In fact, it was the same beautiful face, right down to the perfect skin, the blue-green eyes, and the impish dimple in the left cheek. But although they looked almost exactly alike, Elizabeth and Jessica were as different as night and day. Jessica was the frivolous twin, mainly interested in boys, shopping, and having a good time. Elizabeth, on the other hand, was a serious student who hoped to be a professional writer someday. She preferred spending time with her boyfriend, Todd Wilkins, or one of her few close friends to her sister's hectic social life.

"I know what you mean." Elizabeth laughed. "Sometimes even Todd amazes me."

Maria glanced at April. "Are you and Michael OK?" she asked gently.

April blushed again. "Michael?"

"You don't have to say anything if you don't want to," Elizabeth said quickly. "It's just that sometimes it helps to talk."

April couldn't agree more. But as much as she needed to talk to someone, she felt disloyal discussing Michael—even with someone as nice and as discreet as Elizabeth, and someone who knew him as well as Maria. "I know Todd and Michael are friends," she said to Elizabeth. Then she glanced over at Maria. "And I know you and Michael used to date."

"Date?" Maria grinned. "We were *engaged*."

April hadn't been sure whether or not Maria would want to talk about her engagement to Michael, especially not to April, but she seemed perfectly relaxed about it.

"It was before I started dating Winston," Maria explained. "Michael's father didn't want him to have anything to do with me because of a long-time feud he had with my father. Well, you know Michael." Maria smiled. "His father

11

told him not to see me, so of course we became secretly engaged!"

April couldn't help smiling, too. "Michael can be a little . . . um . . . stubborn."

"At the time I thought Michael and I were really serious," Maria continued, "but now I can see that we weren't. In the end, we just didn't seem to agree on very much." She smiled ruefully. "You're right about his stubbornness. I guess he's a little like his father. Once he gets an idea in his head . . ." She touched April's arm. "Not that he's not a wonderful guy," she added quickly. "Because he is. Complicated, maybe, but really nice."

April couldn't help laughing. "Complicated? Oh, I hadn't noticed that." She bit her lip. She really hated talking about Michael behind his back, but there was one thing she couldn't resist asking Maria. "What about Artie Western?" she said slowly. "Do you know him, too?"

Maria shook her head. "Not really. I've said hello to him once or twice, but that's all." She frowned thoughtfully. "I guess our relationship was supposed to be so hush-hush, Michael didn't really introduce me to his friends. And anyway, I wasn't into the racing scene at all. But from everything I hear, Artie's a great guy."

"He is a great guy," Elizabeth agreed.

April couldn't hide her surprise. A great

12

guy? Artie Western? Not according to Michael, anyway.

They came out of the building and into the sparkling sunlight. "Do you want a ride home?" Maria asked.

"No thanks," April said quickly. "I already have a ride." She watched Maria and Elizabeth disappear around the corner and then started walking in the opposite direction. She didn't have a ride, but she wanted to be by herself for a while.

Todd Wilkins stopped his car in the driveway of the Wakefields' pretty split-level house.

Elizabeth turned to him with a smile. "Why don't you come in for a snack?" she asked. "I don't think anyone else is home yet, and it would be nice to have you to myself for a few more minutes."

Todd leaned over and gave her a kiss. "You want me, you've got me," he said with a grin. "I don't suppose you've got any of your famous homemade chocolate chip cookies?"

Laughing, Elizabeth pushed him away. "I should have known. You don't love me, you love my chocolate chip cookies."

"It's not true," Todd protested, following her out of the car. "I love you *and* I love your chocolate chip cookies!"

Prince Albert, the Wakefields' golden retriever, came bounding up to Elizabeth, his tail wagging enthusiastically as they entered the house. "At least someone loves me for myself," Elizabeth teased.

"That's just because he's never tasted your chocolate chip cookies." Todd put his keys on the table and looked around. "I'll pour us some juice, OK?"

Elizabeth put her books down. "Sure. I'll just get some glasses." She went over to the counter. "Yuck," she said, staring into the sink. "What a disgusting mess."

"What is it?" Todd asked, coming up behind her.

Elizabeth shook her head. "It looks like a primal swamp," she said, holding her nose. "And it smells like one, too."

Todd peered over her shoulder. "The sink's backed up, that's all. There's probably something stuck in the pipe. Don't worry about a thing. Handyman Wilkins is at your service."

With the help of Prince Albert, who insisted on licking his ear through most of the operation, Todd soon located the trouble. One of Jessica's barrettes had fallen down the drain and lodged itself in the U-bend, blocking the pipe. "It's a lucky thing I was here," Todd joked as he flushed the pipe with clean water, "or you wouldn't have known what to do."

Elizabeth passed him a towel for his hands. "Of course I would have known what to do," she said. "I would have called a plumber."

14

"Exactly. And spent a lot of money having something fixed that anyone could have taken care of," Todd said.

Elizabeth had stopped smiling. "You mean anyone but me," she said softly.

Todd finished drying his hands and put the towel back on the rack. "No," he said quickly, "I meant anyone who knew how to do it."

"But not me," she persisted.

Todd put his hands on her shoulders. "Elizabeth," he explained, "all I meant was that you don't know much about plumbing."

Elizabeth glared at him. "And you do?"

Todd gestured with his arms. "I did fix the sink, Liz. You have to admit that I know more about plumbing than you do. I mean, you're a terrific journalist, Elizabeth, but let's face it, you're not very mechanical. Remember the time the Fiat got a flat? Who had to call her boyfriend to come and change the tire for her?"

Elizabeth folded her arms across her chest. "Are you saying I can't change a tire or unclog a sink because I'm a girl?"

"I didn't say that," Todd insisted, "I just said that—"

"Because if that's what you think, Todd Wilkins," Elizabeth continued, "then you'd better think again. There isn't anything you can do that I can't do just as well."

Todd grinned. "And anything you can do, Elizabeth Wakefield, I can do."

Elizabeth couldn't help smiling. "OK," she

15

said. "You're on. Why don't we have a little contest to prove our points? I'll give you a list of three things that I do well, and you'll give me three things that you do well. Whichever of us completes his or her list successfully is the winner."

Todd reached out to shake her hand. "Only if the prize is a special date," he said. "Paid for by the loser."

Elizabeth shook his hand and smiled. "That's fine with me," she said confidently. "We both remember who won the last bet we had." Elizabeth was referring to the time she had decided to pair up Aaron Dallas and Dana Larson. Todd had said that it would never work, but Elizabeth proved him wrong. She smiled at him. "I was just thinking how much I'd like to go back to the Castillo San Angelo for dinner," she teased. "So you'd better start saving your money."

Two

Jessica burst into Elizabeth's room on Friday morning with the grimy barrette Todd had fished out of the kitchen pipe. "Hey," she called, "where did you find this?"

Elizabeth was standing in front of her dresser, brushing her hair. "It was stuck in the kitchen sink."

"Well, thanks," Jessica said. "I've been looking all over for it." She tossed it onto her sister's desk. "Wait till you hear what I've just discovered. It's only the most exciting thing ever!" She held up a magazine for Elizabeth to examine.

"What is that?" Elizabeth asked.

Jessica hurled herself onto the bed. "Isn't it great?" she asked. "Have you ever seen such cool clothes before? Just look at the colors! It's even better than surfing gear."

Elizabeth looked at it more closely. "Jessica," she said, "that looks like a dirt bike magazine."

Jessica looked surprised. "A dirt bike magazine?" she asked. "Why, so it is. And I thought it was a fashion magazine."

But Elizabeth was not in the mood for joking around. "What are you doing with a dirt bike magazine?"

Jessica looked up. "I'm reading it. You're not the only one in this family who can read, you know."

Elizabeth plopped down beside her twin. "You know what I mean, Jess. *Why* are you reading it?"

Jessica gave her sister a look of irritation. "Because it's interesting, Elizabeth, that's why. Is there some law against me reading about something I'm interested in?"

Elizabeth sighed. "Of course there's no law against it," she said. "It's just that, after my motorcycle accident . . . well, I don't think Mom would be too happy if she thought you were getting interested in dirt bike racing." Some time before, Todd had bought a motorcycle, and Mr. and Mrs. Wakefield had forbidden Elizabeth to ride on it. But Elizabeth had disobeyed her parents and gotten in a serious accident. Since then, Mr. and Mrs. Wakefield didn't like to hear the word *motorcycle* mentioned in their presence.

"Oh, come on, Liz," Jessica moaned. "It's

not like I'm going to ride myself. I'm just going to the rally tomorrow to watch. That's all." She tossed back her hair. "There's nothing else exciting happening around here."

Elizabeth narrowed her eyes. "You're just going to watch?"

"Of course I am," Jessica said. "I would never get on a motorbike, knowing how Mom and Dad feel about it."

Elizabeth stared into her sister's face. She certainly looked sincere. But sixteen years of living with Jessica had taught Elizabeth one thing: whenever Jessica said, "I would never . . . ," chances were good that sooner or later she probably would.

"So," Elizabeth said to her parents as she began her breakfast, "then Todd and I came up with the idea of a competition."

"But, honey," Mr. Wakefield said, looking up from his paper, "some people are just better at certain things than other people."

Alice Wakefield raised her eyebrows. "Excuse me, Ned?" she asked politely. "Just what are you trying to say?"

"I'm not talking about men versus women," Mr. Wakefield said quickly. Elizabeth realized that as the only male in the house now that Steven was away at college, her father must sometimes feel a little outnumbered. "I'm talk-

19

ing about people in general. For instance," he said, nodding at Mrs. Wakefield, "I wouldn't expect you to change the oil in the car."

"I wouldn't expect you to, either," Mrs. Wakefield said. "After all, you're the only one who has ever forgotten to put gas in the tank." She glanced at Jessica. "Except for Jessica, that is."

Mr. Wakefield rustled his paper. "Now, Alice . . ."

But Mrs. Wakefield was shaking her head. "Do you remember the time you built the bookshelf and it collapsed in the middle of the night?" she asked with a laugh.

Elizabeth came to her father's rescue. "I know that we're all better at some things than others," she said. "But I also think that men and women have different ideas of what they *can* do based on their sex."

"You mean, you would never think of learning how to unclog a pipe," Mrs. Wakefield said.

Elizabeth nodded. "Exactly. And Todd would never think of learning how to make chocolate chip cookies. That's why we're going to choose things for each other that are out of character."

Mr. Wakefield sipped his coffee thoughtfully. "I see what you're getting at," he said. "Your mother might be a terrific shelf builder, but it wouldn't occur to her to try." He smiled. "Whereas I'm a terrible shelf builder, but because I'm a man I assumed I could do it."

20

Mrs. Wakefield pushed her plate aside. "So," she said excitedly, "what tasks are you going to give Todd?"

As soon as Michael picked her up that morning, April knew there was something wrong.

"What's the matter?" she asked as she climbed into the Trans-Am. "You look really upset."

"I *am* really upset," Michael said. He ran his hand through his hair. "I've got some very bad news," he said quietly, not looking directly into April's eyes.

"Michael," April whispered, "what's wrong?"

He leaned against the steering wheel. "It's my grandmother. You know, the one who lives in Texas."

April nodded. She had heard a lot about this grandmother because she was the only person in the family besides Michael who had ever ridden on a motorbike. She had enjoyed it, too.

Michael breathed deeply. "Well, she's sick. She's in the hospital."

April was immediately concerned. She knew that Michael's grandmother was pretty old, and that she lived by herself. "Oh, no," she said.

Michael turned to face her. "That's not the worst thing, though," he sighed.

April's heart pounded. "Is it really serious?"

He looked slightly puzzled. "No," he said,

shaking his head. "I mean that my parents are making me go with them to see her. Tonight!"

"Well," April said slowly, "I'm sure they're right. It will mean a lot to your grandmother."

"April," Michael said, "don't you understand? They're taking me to Texas. Tonight. I'm going to miss tomorrow's race."

April stared into his hazel eyes. *Now don't misunderstand him*, she told herself. *Remember that he's complicated. Just because he doesn't sound upset that his grandmother is ill doesn't mean that he isn't. This is probably just his way of dealing with the worry. Some people are like that.* She cleared her throat. "But Michael," she said gently, "I bet it'll make your grandmother feel better just to see you."

Michael started up the engine. "April, it's not like she's dying."

"Michael," she replied, "it's not like there won't be another race."

He looked pained. "But without me there, Artie stands a really good chance of winning tomorrow."

"Don't you think you're getting a little carried away about Artie?" April asked.

Michael put the engine into gear and released the hand brake. "No," he said, "I don't think I'm getting a little carried away. This guy gets everything, April. From the time we were little, if Artie wanted something, Artie got it. If I got a bike, Artie got a better bike. If I got a good report card, Artie got a better one. Even when

22

we were riding together, he was always right. He always got his way." He pulled the car into traffic.

"But what about your grandmother?" asked April.

Michael stared at the road ahead. "My grandmother would understand," he said shortly. "She wouldn't want Artie Western to beat me, either."

For all the attention she had paid in her morning classes, April decided, she might as well have stayed home in bed. She had tried to be interested in algebraic equations, but all she could think of was Michael and his obsession with Artie Western. It was in the same half-trance that she entered the cafeteria, got on the lunch line, and began putting food on her tray.

"The salad looks better than usual today, doesn't it?" said a voice beside her.

April looked up to see Cara Walker's smiling face. "Oh, uh, yes," she said.

Cara put some salad on her tray. "Not that I really care what it looks like. By the time lunch period comes around I'm usually hungry enough to eat anything."

April kept staring at Cara. She knew there was something about Cara that she should be remembering. Something important. But except that Cara was funny and nice, April couldn't remember what it was.

"Steven says I eat like a football player."

April smiled. Steven! Of course, that was it! Cara Walker went out with Steven Wakefield. But before Steven, Cara had gone out with none other than Artie Western! If anyone knew about Michael and Artie and what had happened between them, it must be Cara. How could she ask her about it? "You're right," April agreed, deciding that any conversation was better than no conversation. "The salad does look edible." She helped herself to a bowl.

"These sandwiches look pretty good, too," Cara continued, putting a cheese-and-salami hero on her tray.

"Yes," April agreed, "they do, don't they?" She helped herself to a sandwich as well. She was going to have enough food to feed all of southern California before she was able to think of a way of bringing up Artie Western's name.

Cara added a bag of potato chips to her tray with a shake of her head. "It must be because it's Friday," she said, laughing. "Fridays always make me hungry."

April couldn't do it. She couldn't add a bag of potato chips to everything else she had taken. And she couldn't find a subtle way of bringing up Artie. She took a deep breath. "Cara," she said, watching her reach for a brownie, "didn't you used to go out with Artie Western?"

Cara started fumbling in her wallet for money. "That's right," she said. "He's a sweetheart."

24

She gave April a grin. "Not as much of a sweetheart as Steven, of course." She dumped a handful of coins on her tray. "Why?"

April shrugged. "Oh, no reason. It's just that he and Michael used to be friends. . . ."

Cara smiled. "That's right. I'd almost forgotten that. Steven says that Mike and Artie were so close in elementary school that people used to tease them about being twins."

April followed Cara to the table where Jessica, Lila, and Amy were sitting. "So what happened?"

"I don't really know. I don't think Artie ever mentioned it."

"What are we talking about?" asked Jessica, moving over to give April a little more room.

Cara plunked herself down. "Why Artie Western and Mike Harris don't speak to each other anymore."

Jessica nodded. "Oh, them," she said. "Didn't they have a fight over some girl?"

Lila shook her head. "No. I'm sure they fought over a motorcycle or something."

"I think Jessica's right," Cara said. "I think it was a girl." She examined her sandwich. "But I guess it could have been about a bike."

"I remember what it was." Amy shook her head. "You're both wrong. Michael nearly got Artie killed."

Lila snapped her fingers. "No, I remember. It was Artie who nearly got Michael killed."

Jessica looked at April. "Don't listen to

them," she said dismissively. "It was definitely over a girl."

April gazed down at her salad. "Thanks. I'm glad I asked."

That evening, while Michael and his family flew to Texas, April went to the first night of the film festival. She was feeling happy as she hurried down the block to the theater and attached herself to the end of the line. She almost felt relieved that Michael had had to leave town. If she somehow had managed to drag him along, she probably would not have had a very good time.

The line started to move forward, and April moved with it. But when the line stopped, April kept going—right into the person in front of her.

"Oh, I'm sorry," she said as a young man turned around to see what had hit him. "I guess I wasn't looking where I was going."

"That's all right." He laughed. "It wasn't exactly like being hit by a tank."

April couldn't believe her eyes. "Oh . . . um . . . right," she mumbled. She felt her cheeks turn pink. There, right in front of her, was Artie Western.

"Hey, I know you," he said. "You're April Dawson, aren't you? You ride that magenta 125."

"Yes," April said, managing a smile. "Yes, I do. I mean, I am."

He extended his hand. "I'm Artie Western. I've seen you around school and around the track, but I don't think we've ever been introduced."

There was something so straightforward about him that she immediately began to feel at ease. "Hi," she said. "I've seen you around, too."

The line began to move forward again, and they fell into step together. "You a fan?" he asked, nodding toward the poster advertising the film.

"Oh, yes," April said. "I think Hitchcock's probably my favorite director."

"Mine, too." Artie grinned. "I've been looking forward to this series for weeks."

Since they had entered the theater together, it seemed perfectly natural that they should sit together as well. And share a tub of popcorn. And scream together through the scary parts.

"Well, what did you think?" he asked as they reemerged into the night after the film.

"It was great. I loved it," April said enthusiastically.

Artie nodded. "I loved it, too. I'll never look at a pigeon the same way again." He laughed. "Hey, do you feel like joining me for a pizza?"

April's first instinct was to say no. She knew

Michael would not approve. In fact, Michael would be furious. On the other hand, April reasoned, Michael had no right to choose her friends for her. And besides, if she got to know Artie a little better, she might be able to find out what had happened between him and Michael. April smiled. "That sounds great."

On the way to Guido's they talked about the movie. But as they had ordered, Artie turned to her with a serious expression. "So, how's he doing?"

"How's who doing?" April asked, her mind still on the film.

"Mike," Artie said immediately. "I've been wanting to ask you all night."

April continued to stare at him blankly. "Mike?" she repeated. "You want to know how Mike is?"

"You are Mike's girlfriend, aren't you?"

April nodded, feeling a little embarrassed. She had never expected Artie to bring up Michael so casually, as though they were still friends. "Oh, yes," she said quickly. "Yes, I am."

Artie smiled. "I'm glad he's with someone as nice as you," he said simply.

April fumbled with her napkin. "He's doing fine. You know Mike," she said with a little laugh. "As long as his bike's running, he's happy."

Artie nodded. "Yeah," he said, helping himself to a slice of pizza. "I know Mike." A look of genuine admiration came into his eyes. "Mike's a great rider and an excellent mechanic. It wouldn't surprise me if he became a professional."

April sprinkled hot-pepper flakes on her pizza and waited for Artie to tell her what had happened between them. She even asked him several leading questions about how long he and Mike had ridden together and what prizes they had won, but Artie answered briefly and changed the subject. Finally April decided to come right out with it. She took a deep breath. "So, why did you two stop riding together?"

Artie sat up straight and looked right at her. "April," he said, "if you don't mind, I'd really rather not talk about it, OK? The past is the past. Let's just say that we had a misunderstanding and we were both at fault."

April nodded. "Sure. I didn't mean to be nosy."

"Have some more pizza," Artie urged. "We bikers have to keep up our strength."

April smiled, but inside she was even more confused. Whatever had happened, Michael didn't think it was a misunderstanding. And he certainly didn't think it was both their faults.

Usually, the last thing Elizabeth and Todd did when they said goodnight was exchange a kiss. Usually, but not that night. That night they exchanged envelopes.

29

"I think I like the kiss better," Todd joked, taking a pale blue envelope from Elizabeth and giving her a white one. The envelopes contained the lists of tasks they had made up for each other.

Elizabeth laughed. "Should we look at them now? Or would you prefer to be in the privacy of your own room when you realize I'm going to win?"

Todd grinned. "Actually, it's your delicate feelings I'm worried about," he teased. "You know how I hate to see you cry."

They tore open the envelopes. "Well?" Todd asked. "What do you think?"

Elizabeth read her list out loud. " 'Change a tire, build a shelf, and replace a washer.' That's it? I'll probably be done in an hour."

Todd read his list. " 'Do the grocery shopping for a week, make an apron, and cook Elizabeth Wakefield's dinner, including chocolate chip cookies.' " He snapped his fingers. "This is going to be like taking candy from a baby, Elizabeth. A sleeping baby. Are you sure you don't want to call the whole thing off?"

Elizabeth stepped into the house. "Don't forget I like walnuts in my chocolate chip cookies," she said as the door shut behind her.

Three

"It's for you, April," called Mrs. Dawson, holding out the receiver.

April's first thought was that it must be Michael, calling to tell her how his grandmother was doing. "Hello?"

"Hi." The voice on the other end was male, but it wasn't Michael's. "It's me, Artie."

"Artie?" She couldn't hide her surprise.

"I hope you don't mind me calling," he said. "I got your number from the rally roster."

"Of course I don't mind," April assured him. "What's up?"

He laughed. "Well, that's just it. Nothing's up. Pete, my partner, has come down with the flu, so I've got no one to ride with today." He cleared his throat. "And since you mentioned

Michael was away, I was wondering if you'd want to ride together."

"Ride with *you?*"

"It just seemed silly to me that neither of us was going to enter because we didn't have partners," Artie explained. "I mean, it is a relay, and the course is similar to the one we'll be covering in the championship in a couple of weeks. The practice could do us both good."

April couldn't believe her ears. "I don't get it," she said. "I'm a competitor, Artie. Why would you want me to benefit from practice?"

"Why not?" he asked. "Anyway, I need the practice, too."

Why not? Because of what Michael would say, April thought. But as she thought more about it, it did seem a shame that neither of them was going to race because they didn't have partners. Besides, the practice would be good for her. And, of course, it would give her another opportunity to figure out what had happened between Artie and Michael. "OK," April said quickly before she had time to think about what Michael's reaction would be. She laughed nervously. "You've got yourself a teammate."

Jessica stared at herself in her full-length mirror trying to decide what to wear to the dirt bike rally. She frowned at her reflection. The trouble was, there wasn't anyone she could ask. Most of her friends were into surfing and shopping—not bumping over rocky ground on a motorbike. Elizabeth would just give her a hard time about going at all, and asking her mother, of course, was out of the question.

Jessica looked at the pile of rejected outfits already on the floor. Maybe she should try on that short white skirt again. She made a disgusted face. The white skirt made her look as though she was planning to play tennis. Next she tried on a pair of flowered shorts that made her look like she was going to a luau. She collapsed on her bed, and flicked through the magazine she had bought. The photographs centered on the bikers or the ground they were sailing over, but there was no hint as to how the spectators dressed.

Finally Jessica decided on a pair of bright pink shorts and a blue T-shirt. At least she wouldn't blend into the trees. She gave herself one last look in the mirror. The colors did set off her eyes and her hair. And they went well with the bright colors the bikers seemed to wear. Yes, she would fit in and stand out at the same time.

Jessica hurried out of the house toward the driveway, where the Fiat was parked. Next to the Fiat was her brother Steven's car, and kneeling on the dirty pavement were Steven, who was home from college for the weekend, and Elizabeth. For some reason her twin seemed to be trying to pry off a hubcap.

"Elizabeth!" Jessica exclaimed. "What are you doing?"

Steven grinned. "I'm showing Liz how to change a tire," he said. He patted his sister's shoulder. "She's doing very well, too."

"I'm not so sure," Elizabeth said with a chuckle. "It took me thirty minutes just to jack up the car. Now if I could only get this hubcap off . . ."

Jessica put her hands on her hips. "I don't believe this," she said. "Elizabeth, you're absolutely filthy! You're going to end up with the hands of a mechanic."

Steven shook his head. "You know, it wouldn't be such a bad idea for you to learn how to do this, too, Jessica. After all, you drive the Fiat as much as Elizabeth. What would you do if you got a flat while you were all by yourself?"

Jessica laughed. "Well, that's easy," she said with a toss of her head. "I'd wait till some cute boy came along and I'd get him to fix it for me!"

"You're pretty confident with the line we've decided on, aren't you?" Artie asked April.

April nodded. Right then, she was pretty confident about everything. They had come out to the course early to work out their strategy and get a feel for the terrain. Artie was so thorough and competent that she was sure they

34

stood a good chance of winning. "Absolutely," she said. "And I'm very happy about taking the second half."

"I know how you ride," Artie said, "and I'm sure that between the two of us you're the better driver for that part."

As important as his thoroughness, however, was his easygoing nature. With Michael it was always, "Did you do this, April? Did you do that?" The night before a race he would phone her half a dozen times, making sure that she hadn't forgotten anything. It drove her crazy. It drove her mother crazy, too. "What's wrong with that boy?" Mrs. Dawson would ask. "How many times does he think he has to tell you the same thing?" On the day of a race Michael usually had her out at the track at the crack of dawn, and he wouldn't stop nagging her until they were ready to start. Working with Artie was totally different. He knew she was a good and experienced rider and he assumed she would do the best she could, which made her feel relaxed and sure of herself. April sighed. To be fair to Michael, he was as hard on himself as he was on her. Sometimes she wondered if either of them could ever meet his standards.

"A spark plug for your thoughts," Artie said with a smile.

April blinked, suddenly aware that she hadn't heard anything he'd said for the last few minutes. "Oh, Artie, I'm sorry. I was just thinking about Michael."

He nodded. "I thought you might be. I guess it'll be pretty strange for you, riding with someone else."

"Yes," said April, feeling a rush of excitement about racing that she hadn't felt in some time. "It'll be pretty strange."

Jessica had known that the rally was not going to be held in a stadium. That much had been clear from her magazine. But she hadn't realized the races were run on the land around the lake. It couldn't even be called a trail, really. It was just woods and hills and rocky ground. Jessica imagined that zipping around the lake was pretty scenic for the contestants, but for the onlookers it meant they could only see part of each race. Sometimes the races didn't even start and end in the same place!

Jessica was standing near the finish line. It was boring. There seemed to be a very long gap between the end of one race and the beginning of the next one. At most sporting events she had attended, there was at least music to listen to or cheerleaders to watch. Here, the only other thing to do was watch boys fooling around with their bikes, talking about their bikes, and comparing their bikes. Next to this, lunch with Lila, Amy, and Cara was a thrilling event.

Jessica leaned against a tree with a sigh. She was sure that some of the racers must be cute, at least. After all, Michael Harris and Artie Western were both good-looking. The trouble was that though the bikers wore clothes that were definitely cool, their bodies were completely covered. Once they put their helmets on, their own mothers wouldn't have been able to tell them apart. Jessica yawned. That was what she liked about surfing: not only could she see everything that was happening, she could also see who was making it happen. Just then a group of bikers flashed past her amid the cheers of the crowd. A little shiver ran through her. The racing itself—the little bit she could see of it—was actually pretty exciting. And some of the jumps and turns were really breathtaking.

Jessica took her program out of her bag. Unless she had fallen asleep standing up—which was not completely impossible—the next event was the one April and Michael were in. Jessica cheered up a little. There was a refreshment stand not far away; she decided she would go and get herself a drink and a snack, and then she would start looking out for April's magenta bike to come over the rise.

As she stood there a few minutes later, eating a taco, Jessica felt as though she'd been looking for April for hours. Every now and then she would hear clapping and cheering in the distance, but in front of her there was nothing but sky, road, and trees. And then something sparkled in the distance. Way ahead of the other contestants, two bikes were bearing down on the finish line. As they came a little closer, Jessica could see that one was metallic blue and the other was a startling magenta. Suddenly Jessica understood what the fascination of this sport was all about. The little shivers she had felt watching the earlier races were nothing compared to the thrill that ran through her when she saw April's bike practically fly over the hill. There might be no way of recognizing her friend under her layers of protective clothing and her helmet, but there was no way of mistaking that bright pink bike. Jessica started jumping up and down, almost as though she were leading a cheer. "Come on, April!" she shouted. "Come on, April! Show them what you've got!" Several people around her began shouting as well. The blue bike pushed forward, dipping around a sharp bend, but April was right behind it. The crowd roared. Jessica was beside herself with excitement. "April!" she screamed. "Don't let him beat you! April, come on!" The pink bike streaked across the finish line, with the blue bike just behind, and the crowd burst into applause. Flushed and breathless, Jessica turned to the people next to her. "That's my friend April," she informed them. "The girl on the magenta bike. Isn't she great?"

As soon as she could, Jessica hurried over to congratulate April on a wonderful race. She assumed that the young man in the red-and-white racing suit who had rushed up to hug April was Michael, but when he turned around she realized that it wasn't Michael Harris at all. It was Artie Western! "What happened to Michael?" she asked April after she had congratulated her. "I thought you always raced with him."

April explained that Michael had had to go visit his grandmother in Texas at the last minute. But then Artie came back, and April didn't finish.

Jessica guessed that the argument between the two boys had been resolved, and that Artie had offered to take Michael's place while he was away.

A few minutes later, Jessica pulled the Fiat into the parking lot of the Dairi Burger. April and Artie had invited her to join them and a few others for a victory hamburger and milkshake.

Jessica had hesitated about the invitation. She was a little worried that a bunch of dirt bikers sitting around a table together might talk about nothing but stutter bumps and shock absorbers. That's about all the magazine had talked about. And worse yet, what if her mother drove by the Dairi Burger and saw her sitting with all these bikers? It might be a little difficult to explain.

"Oh, come on, Jessica," April had pleaded. "It'll be fun."

Jessica got out of her car and went inside.

She hoped April was right, and she hoped her mother wasn't cruising around Sweet Valley, looking to see if her daughter was hanging out with kids in helmets and chest protectors.

The others were already at a table at the back. Much to her relief, none of them was wearing a helmet or a chest protector. In fact, they looked like an average group of hamburger-eating teenagers. Her mother would never suspect a thing.

"Jessica!" April called. "Jessica! Over here!"

Jessica waved.

"Sam," April ordered the boy sitting across from her, "move over and let Jessica sit next to you."

"Sure thing," said Sam as he slid over. He turned to Jessica with a smile. "Hi," he said. "I'm Sam Woodruff."

For one of the few times since she had first learned to talk, Jessica was speechless. Sam Woodruff was just about the handsomest boy she had ever seen. Ever. He was lean and blond with thick, curly hair, light gray eyes, and fine features.

Jessica recovered herself quickly. "Hi." She smiled back. "I'm Jessica Wakefield."

"Do you go to school with April and Artie?" he asked.

Jessica nodded, still finding it difficult to speak. "That's right. Where do you go to school?"

"I'm a senior at Bridgewater." He seemed

to be staring right into her eyes. "I haven't seen you around before. Are you a racer, too?"

"No," Jessica admitted, trying to sound unhappy about it. "No, I'm not a dirt biker. I'm a cheerleader."

"A cheerleader?" Sam laughed. It was the warmest laugh she had ever heard. "Do you mean that you actually *understand* football?" He shook his head. "My father used to take me to games when I was little. The whole stadium would be on its feet, cheering, and I'd be curled up on the bleacher, sound asleep."

Good-looking and a sense of humor, Jessica thought. And he didn't understand football, either. There was nothing worse than going out with a boy who wanted to talk about football all the time. "I bet you wouldn't fall asleep if you went to a game with me," she joked.

"No," he said softly, "I bet I wouldn't."

She could feel her face turn red. She pushed back a strand of hair.

"I might take you up on that offer." Sam grinned.

Jessica grinned back. *You will if I have anything to do with it*, she said to herself.

"So?" Todd asked as he and Elizabeth took their seats in the movie theater. "How have you been doing with your tasks?"

Elizabeth reached over and took a handful of popcorn. "Not too badly. I got a little dirty, but

41

I did manage to get the tire changed eventually." She decided not to mention that she would never have been able to do it if she had not had Steven helping her. Or that she wasn't sure she would actually be willing to drive on the tire she had changed.

Todd leaned over and gave her a kiss on the cheek. "I'm impressed," he said. "I have to confess I wasn't really sure you'd be able to do it. It isn't the easiest job."

"It's all in knowing how," Elizabeth said with more assurance than she actually felt. "And what about you? Did you get your family's shopping done?"

Todd waved his hand as though chasing away a gnat. "Nothing to it," he said airily. "In one door and out the other. I don't know why my parents always complain about it so much."

"Well, I wouldn't get too confident if I were you," Elizabeth teased. "The first task was practically a gift. They get harder after that."

Todd put his arm around her shoulders. "The same goes for you, my pretty," he said in an evil-sounding voice. "The same goes for you."

Four

On Monday morning Jessica stomped into the bathroom where her sister was getting ready for school. She slammed the door behind her and threw herself against the towel rack in a gesture of despair. "That's it!" she announced dramatically. "I've had it with the opposite sex. I'm going to devote my life to doing good works and forget about men forever."

Elizabeth glanced at her sister in the mirror, unable to suppress a smile.

"Don't look at me like that," Jessica ordered, catching sight of Elizabeth's reflection. She stuck out her tongue. "This time I really mean it. I have never been so disappointed in my life."

Elizabeth reached for a towel. "What's the matter?" she teased. "Weren't there any cute boys at that rally?"

Jessica threw her hands in the air. "Why do I bother talking to you?" she groaned. "You obviously never listen to a word I say."

Elizabeth became serious. Jessica did look upset. And it was true that Elizabeth had been so preoccupied with beating Todd in their contest that she hadn't really been paying much attention to her sister the past weekend. She had a vague memory that Jessica had come back from the rally very excited, but she couldn't quite remember why. "That's not true, Jess," she said sincerely. "It's just that I've had a lot on my mind this weekend."

"Tires," said Jessica. "Your only sister's life is falling apart and all you can think about is changing tires."

"I'm listening now," Elizabeth said. "Tell me what happened."

"Nothing happened," she said glumly. "That's the trouble. A big fat nothing." Jessica sat down on the edge of the tub. There was a catch in her voice when she continued. "I waited all Saturday night and all day yesterday, and he never called."

"Who never called?" Elizabeth asked gently.

"Sam Woodruff, the most incredible boy I've ever met." She kicked the bathtub. "I know he really liked me. I just know he did."

"When exactly did he say he'd call?" Elizabeth asked.

"What?"

"When did he say he'd call? I mean, maybe

he couldn't get to a telephone, or something came up."

Jessica rolled her eyes. "I don't believe this. You don't even know him and already you're taking his side."

"I'm not taking his side," Elizabeth said. "All I asked was when he said he'd call you."

Jessica looked at her feet. "He didn't say exactly."

"But you gave him your number—"

Jessica shook her head. "No, I didn't give him my number. We got so involved in talking to each other that I guess he just forgot to ask."

"Let me get this straight," Elizabeth said slowly. "You didn't give him your number, he never said he'd call, but you're angry because he didn't call."

Jessica got to her feet. "I'm not *angry*, Liz," she said as she started back to her room. "I'm hurt, I'm heartbroken, and I'm going to go to Tibet and live in a cave for the rest of my life, but I wouldn't say that I was *angry*." She shook her head. "You know I love you, Liz, but sometimes I find it very hard to understand how you think."

Elizabeth watched Jessica disappear into the disaster area she called her room. "I know just what you mean," she said to herself.

By the time she arrived at school, Jessica was feeling one hundred percent better. Elizabeth was right, she had decided. Sam hadn't said when he would call, and she hadn't given him her number, so it would probably take him a little time to get in touch. He'd probably have to call April or Artie to get her number, and maybe he felt a little shy about it. Maybe he was waiting till he bumped into one of them at a race or something. Jessica sailed into Sweet Valley High with a spring in her step. *That's it,* she told herself. *He'll be calling me in a few days.* She didn't have to move to Tibet after all.

Jessica stopped short in the hallway. There, right in front of her, getting his books from his locker, was the person who might very well be the answer to her prayers: Michael Harris. In the past, Jessica had never said more than a few words to Michael, most of them being "Hi" or "Do you know what the history homework is?" But things had changed. If April and Artie were friends with Sam, Jessica figured, then Michael was probably a friend of his, too. He could put in a good word for her. He could even give Sam her phone number.

"Mike!" she called, hurrying up to him.

Michael turned around. "Oh, hi, Jessica," he said, smiling.

"April told me about your grandmother. How's she doing?"

"She's better, thanks," Michael answered. "My mom stayed in Texas to keep an eye on her, and my dad and sister and I came back home."

"Well, that's good news," Jessica said sin-

46

cerely. She tugged at a strand of her hair. "It's too bad you missed the rally on Saturday," she went on. "April and Artie were really terrific, but I'm sure they weren't nearly as good as you and April usually are."

No sooner were the words out of her mouth then Jessica realized she had said the wrong thing. Michael's eyes darkened and his face turned red. His smile looked like it had been set in cement.

"April and Artie?" he repeated.

They were still at war, Jessica realized, and here she was, standing in the middle of the battlefield, shooting off her big mouth. "It was my first rally," she said brightly, trying to back away without seeming to, "and I really enjoyed it."

"April and Artie?" Michael repeated. "Are you saying that April and Artie raced *together* on Saturday?"

Jessica was saved by the sudden arrival of Ken Matthews.

"Hey, Mike," Ken greeted him. "I ran into Artie and April at Guido's Friday night." He punched Michael in the arm. "I just wanted to say that I'm really glad you two guys finally patched things up. It hasn't been the same since you stopped speaking to each other."

Michael's eyes, which had been boring into Jessica's, now turned on Ken. "What?"

Jessica felt responsible for having started this, and now it was up to her to end it. Fast.

"That's right," she said quickly. "There was a whole bunch of us at Guido's Friday and Artie happened to sit down at our table." She grabbed Ken's arm. "Isn't that right, Ken?" she asked, squeezing him hard.

"Ow," Ken said. "Jessica, what are you talking about? You're cutting off my circulation."

But Jessica was already dragging him away. "Well, see you, Mike," she said loudly. "Ken and I are going to be late for class. We wouldn't want to be late, would we, Ken?" she shouted, and with that she gave one hard yank and they disappeared around the corner.

The first person April saw when she reached the cafeteria at lunchtime was Michael. He was standing next to the entrance with his arms folded across his chest. He was tapping his foot.

April's heart sank. He had found out about Saturday. She had planned to tell him herself as soon as she had a chance, but she knew from the furious look on his face that she was too late. She realized she should have told him that morning on the way to school, but he'd been so happy to see her, and so relieved that his grandmother was all right, that she hadn't been able to work the conversation around to Artie Western.

He spotted her almost immediately. "I want to talk to you," he called, walking toward her.

"Sure," she answered as calmly as she could. "What is it?"

He pointed to the door. "Outside," he said.

April's heart sank a little lower. He was really angry. He probably wouldn't listen to her side of the story at all. "Michael," she said firmly, "if you'll just give me a chance, I can explain everything."

He grabbed her arm. "You've already made me look like a fool in front of the entire school," he hissed. "I don't want them to hear everything I have to say."

April pulled herself free. "Fine," she said, turning toward the exit. "Outside."

April wasn't sure that being outside really helped. Michael was so angry that it seemed likely the entire population of Sweet Valley could hear every word he said. He paced back and forth at the edge of the football field, shaking his fist in the air. "How could you do this to me?" he shouted. "How could you betray me like this?"

"But I haven't betrayed you," she protested.

Michael kicked a rock across the nine-yard line. "You go out with my worst enemy—you *race* with my worst enemy—and you say you haven't betrayed me?"

"Michael," she said evenly, "if you'd just give me a chance to explain—"

"What is it?" he roared. "Do you think he's smarter or better-looking than I am? Do you think he's a better rider? Do you think he's a nicer person? Is that it, April?" He banged his fist against the goalpost. "Why, April?" he asked, his voice suddenly quiet. "Why did you do this to me?"

She went over to him. "Listen to me, Michael," she said gently. "I didn't do anything to you. I bumped into Artie at the film festival and we started talking. Then after the movie we went for pizza, and then I went home. He knew I didn't have a partner for the race, and the next day he asked me if I'd stand in for his partner, who had the flu. I thought it would be good practice for the championship. I thought you'd be pleased, Michael. You're so determined to win, I figured you'd be happy that I was getting the extra practice."

"Oh, sure you did," Michael snapped. He turned around, shaking his head. "You really amaze me, April. You really do. You become best friends with Artie Western while I'm out of town and you expect me to believe that you did it to make *me* happy? The only thing that would make me happy would be if Artie Western moved to Australia."

April raised her eyes to his. "Do you want the truth, Michael? The truth is that I can't understand why you hate Artie. I thought that maybe if I could find out—"

He pushed past her. "Just leave me alone, April. All right? You don't know anything about what happened, so just mind your own business."

She strode after him. "I know I don't know what happened," she shouted at his back. "Because *you* won't tell me. You and your stupid pride. If only you'd let me help . . ."

"Do you want to help me?" he shouted. "Then stay away from Artie Western. You're either with me or against me, April," he yelled. "Which is it going to be?"

April stood there on the grass, looking at Michael. There was no way of reasoning with him, not in the mood he was in just then. The California sun might be shining everywhere else in Sweet Valley, but he stood under an enormous black cloud. "OK, Michael," she said at last. "I'll stay away from Artie Western, if that's what you want."

Michael nodded. "That's what I want."

"You're a fool, April Dawson," April told her reflection in her dresser mirror. "A complete fool." Ever since she'd come home from school she had been thinking about her argument with Michael on the football field. At the time she would have said anything to get him to stop yelling, but now she wondered if she had made a terrible mistake.

Her reflection frowned back at her. *I'm not a fool*, it seemed to be saying. *I did what I thought was best at the time. I just wanted us to stop fighting.*

"So you gave in?" she demanded, waving

her hairbrush. "You let Michael tell you what to do?"

Her reflection looked a little shamefaced.

April shook the brush again. "No!" she shouted. "Michael and I are equals in everything. Even in dirt bike racing. Who is he to boss me around?"

Her reflection had no answer to this. Everything April had said was true. She and Michael were equals and always had been, even on the track.

"You see!" said April. "I'm right and you know it." She threw the hairbrush on the top of her dresser.

"April?" said a voice behind her. "I've been knocking, but you didn't hear me."

April spun around to find her mother looking at her curiously.

"I thought I heard you talking to someone," her mother said, her eyes darting around the room.

"Oh, Mom." April smiled. "I was just . . . um . . . brushing my hair." She held up the hairbrush for her mother to see.

Mrs. Dawson looked a little relieved. "There's a phone call for you, honey," she said. "It's Mike."

April marched to the telephone. But instead of being the demanding, arrogant tyrant she had been expecting, Michael sounded completely miserable. "April?" he said. "I was afraid you were going to refuse to speak to me."

She had never heard him sound so down. "You were?"

"Not that I'd blame you," he said quickly. "I know you think I'm being irrational and bossy, and you're probably right."

"I am?"

"But I can't help it, April. I really can't. Just the thought of you hanging out with Artie makes me crazy. I just . . . I don't know, I just can't help the way I feel. I'd rather give him my bike and never ride again than have him take you away from me."

April had a sudden urge to hug him. "Michael, Artie's not trying to take me away from you. I wish you would believe that. It's really you he's concerned about."

"Me?" There was something in his voice she had never heard before. "He asked about me? What did he want to know?"

"He wanted to know how you are," April explained. "He said lots of nice things about you."

Michael cleared his throat. "You're making this up, aren't you, April? You're just trying to make me feel better."

Suddenly she knew what she was hearing in his voice. It was sadness. Sadness and loss. "No, Michael," she said, trying to make him believe her. "I'm not making it up." Somehow it had never occurred to her that Michael's dislike of Artie hid so much pain.

Jessica looked up as her mother poked her head through her bedroom door.

Jessica smiled. "Hi, Mom. What's up?"

Mrs. Wakefield held up the plastic garbage bag she was carrying. "It's that time of year again, Jessica," she said with a smile. "Time to empty your wastebasket and clear the plates and glasses from under your bed."

Mrs. Wakefield looked at the floor, which was covered with heaps of clothes and magazines. "Jessica, sometimes I suspect that your possessions are actually capable of breeding. Your blue sweater will mate with your yellow sweater, and the next thing you know you'll have a green sweater, two pairs of socks, and a scarf. What other explanation could there be for the amount of *things* that build up in here?"

Jessica laughed and put her history book down. She had given in and started doing her homework because she was tired of waiting for Sam Woodruff to call her. "Didn't we just do this?" she asked, but she got off the bed without any further argument. As far as Jessica was concerned, even straightening up her room was better than doing her history reading.

54

She started gathering things from under the furniture.

"Jessica," Mrs. Wakefield said, in a tone of voice Jessica recognized instantly. It meant that Jessica was in trouble. "What is this?"

Jessica turned around. Mrs. Wakefield was standing by her dresser, holding the dirt bike magazine Jessica had thrown away that evening in a fit of frustration when Sam hadn't called.

"It's a magazine," she said, putting on an innocent face.

"Don't tell me you're getting interested in motorcycles," Mrs. Wakefield said.

Jessica laughed. "Of course not, Mom, someone at school gave it to me. And anyway, those aren't motorcycles, they're dirt bikes."

"Well, they look the same to me," her mother continued. "You know how your father and I feel about motorcycles. They're terribly dangerous, and after Elizabeth's accident . . . just the sight of them upsets me."

"Mom," Jessica said, "can you really picture me on a dirt bike? You can't wear shorts or bathing suits; you have to wear all this padding."

Mrs. Wakefield looked down at the cover of the magazine.

"Can you imagine *me* wearing a helmet?" Jessica continued. "Mom, do you know what wearing a helmet does to your hair?" Jessica knew that her mother understood how important her clothes and hair were to her.

Mrs. Wakefield stood there, considering. "No," she said. She tossed the magazine back into the wastebasket. "No, I guess I can't."

Jessica flopped back on her bed as soon as her mother left. *Whew,* she said to herself, *that was close.* She hadn't even done anything and she'd almost gotten caught! She sighed. It was probably just as well that she might never see Sam Woodruff again. Her mother would be a lot happier knowing Jessica was safe in a cave in Tibet rather than going out with a dirt biker. As far as Mrs. Wakefield was concerned, if Jessica was going out with a dirt biker, she was going to want to ride a dirt bike, too. After all, Elizabeth would never have gone on a motorcycle if it hadn't belonged to Todd. Yes, it was a good thing that Sam hadn't called, because her parents probably wouldn't let her see him anyway. She closed her eyes and pictured Sam Woodruff's face. Her heart did a little flip-flop. She opened her eyes again. How could he not call her?

From somewhere under a heap of clothes the telephone began to ring. Jessica leaned over the bed and found the receiver. "Hello?" she snapped.

"Hello," said an unsure voice. "May I speak to Jessica Wakefield, please?"

Jessica sat up. "This is Jessica," she said in a much friendlier voice. Suddenly she felt flushed, and her heart was racing.

"Hi, Jessica, this is Sam Woodruff. I don't know if you remember me. . . ."

"Sam Woodruff," Jessica said slowly, somehow managing to sound casual. "Oh, sure. Didn't we meet at the Dairi Burger the other day?"

She could hear the relief in his voice. "That's right." He laughed nervously. "It's taken me ages to track down your phone number. I . . . you . . . well, anyway, it's taken me ages." He laughed again. "Anyway, I was wondering if maybe you'd want to go out with me one night this week?"

"This week?" asked Jessica, pretending she needed to consider it. She didn't believe in seeming too eager, not even when she wanted to scream with joy. "What night did you have in mind?"

There was a second's pause, and then he said, "How about tomorrow?"

She rustled a few pages of her history text, as though she were checking her date book. "Tomorrow?" she repeated. "Yeah, that seems OK."

"Great! I'll pick you up at seven, if that's all right with you."

Pick her up at seven? An image of Sam riding up to the Wakefields' house on his dirt bike suddenly came into her mind. No, there was no way she could let him pick her up and run the risk of him meeting her parents. "I've got a better idea. Why don't I meet you at Guido's?"

"OK," said Sam happily. "Seven o'clock at Guido's. See you tomorrow."

"See you tomorrow," Jessica said, barely containing her excitement.

As soon as she hung up the phone she jumped up and screamed with joy.

Five

Tuesday afternoon after school Elizabeth Wakefield and Enid Rollins, her best friend, found themselves standing outside the lumber and hardware store, staring at the door.

"I don't know about this," Enid said. "I don't see any women in there."

"No," said Elizabeth slowly. "I don't see any, either. But that's because it's used mainly by professional builders. It doesn't mean we can't go in."

"Oh, no, of course not," Enid said quickly. "I mean, it's just a store, isn't it? They can't refuse to let us in just because we're girls."

"Exactly," Elizabeth agreed. "It's just a store." She held tight to the book in her hand, *The ABC's of Do-It-Yourself*. She had gotten it out of the library that afternoon. It contained an entire

59

chapter on putting up shelves. Although Elizabeth had only glanced at it, it didn't seem that hard. All she had to do was nail a couple of brackets into the wall, attach a piece of wood, and she'd be done!

Still, Elizabeth hesitated at the door. Several busy-looking men in work clothes came out, and several more went in. They all seemed to have either a screwdriver sticking out of one pocket or a pencil stuck behind an ear.

Enid sighed. "You know, ever since my parents got divorced, my mother's learned to live without things like shelves. And when the light fixture in the hallway short-circuited, she had to hire some guy to replace it."

"You see?" Elizabeth said. "That's exactly what I mean. There's no reason why your mother couldn't have done that herself; it's just that she's never learned how." She tugged on Enid's sleeve. "Come on. We're going in."

This was not the kind of hardware store that either Elizabeth or Enid was used to. There was no aisle filled with things for the kitchen, no display of colorful plastic dishes or shelf liners. Instead there were barrels and boxes of nails and screws, rows of unfamiliar-looking tools and fixtures, and sawdust on the floor. And there were no women, except for them.

"There aren't even any salesladies," Enid whispered.

"Oh, Enid," Elizabeth hissed back, and pulled

her friend over to the counter with her. "So what?"

Although not a professional shopper like her sister, Elizabeth had been in enough stores in her life to know that there were usually salespeople around to help customers find what they wanted or give them advice.

But not in this store. Elizabeth and Enid waited at the counter for ten minutes before one of the salesmen finally spoke to them.

"Yeah?" he said. "Did you want something?"

Elizabeth stood up straight. "Well, yes. I want to put up a shelf in the kitchen."

The salesman stared back at her.

"For cookbooks," Enid added.

The salesman stared at Enid.

Elizabeth held out her hands as though holding a board between them. "I thought it should be about this long," she explained. "But I'm not sure what type of wood would be best. Is there one type of wood that's better for kitchen shelves than the others?"

"It depends," said the salesman.

"Oh," said Elizabeth, a little surprised at how unfriendly he had made those two words sound. "On what?" she asked bravely.

"On what you want," said the salesman. He just stared at her for a few seconds, and then he said, "What do you want?"

"Well . . ." mumbled Elizabeth.

"I don't think it should be too thick," put in

Enid. She turned to Elizabeth. "It might not go with the style of your kitchen if it were too thick." She turned to the salesman with a smile. "Is that what you mean?"

The salesman seemed to be considering this question. Elizabeth and Enid smiled at him expectantly.

"Rawl plugs or toggle bolts?" the salesman growled.

Elizabeth and Enid exchanged a horrified look. He might as well have asked, "Snakes or sea urchins?" for all they knew. Without another word, Elizabeth and Enid backed toward the door.

April had spent quite a few sleepless hours the previous night worrying about Michael. She knew that she couldn't go on with him the way he was, tense and obsessive. She didn't think that he could, either. Because it wasn't Artie Western who was Michael's worst enemy, it was Michael Harris. She had to help him, whether he wanted her to help him or not. She had to save him from himself. And the perfect plan had come to her just as she was falling asleep.

Part one of Operation Rescue Michael was to make him relax more and not take things so seriously. She needed to get him to laugh and have fun.

So on Tuesday afternoon, as he was driving

her home, she leaned her head against his shoulder and said, "Mike, a bunch of people are going bowling tonight. Why don't we go along?"

"Bowling?" Michael asked. He sounded as though she had suggested that they go ice fishing on Secca Lake—in their bathing suits.

April suppressed a sigh. "Yeah," she said enthusiastically, "bowling. Terri Adams and Ken Matthews always go. Terri says they have a great time."

Michael shook his head. "I'm no good at bowling."

She gave his arm a little squeeze. "Michael, it doesn't matter whether you're good at it or not, it's just a game. Everybody just goes to fool around. You know, to have fun."

"We can have fun doing something else," protested Michael. "We don't have to go bowling."

"OK," said April. "What do you want to do instead?"

"Well, I wanted to check the suspension on your bike—"

"That's it?" April said, trying hard to remember her resolve and not to lose her temper. "You want to work on my bike?"

"The championship isn't that far away, you know. Everything's got to be perfect."

April crossed her arms over her chest. Already she was feeling a lot more like murdering him than rescuing him. "Well," she said, "fun definitely isn't *your* middle name."

Michael stopped the car in front of her house. "No," he said with a grin, "it's Lloyd."

It took Jessica an hour and a half to get ready for her date with Sam. She checked herself one last time in her full-length mirror. She looked terrific, if she said so herself.

"Big date?" asked Mrs. Wakefield, suddenly appearing in the doorway.

Why didn't her mother ever stay in one place anymore, Jessica wondered. She always seemed to be tiptoeing around the house, going through wastebaskets or checking on what Jessica was wearing.

Jessica shrugged. "Oh, no, not really. I'm just meeting some people at Guido's." That wasn't really a lie, she assured herself. Guido's was one of the most popular places in town, and she always ran into someone she knew there.

"That's nice," Mrs. Wakefield said. "Have a good time."

Jessica smiled. "I'll try."

As it turned out, Jessica didn't have to try too hard to have a good time. From the moment she walked in and saw Sam waiting for her in a corner booth she knew it was going to be one of the best nights of her life. He was even cuter than she had remembered, and he was a terrific dresser. She'd been a little worried that he might look like a biker, but he looked so normal that even her mother would have approved. Sam was as bright and funny as he was handsome. It seemed to her that they were made for each other.

Right from the start they began to discover how much they had in common. They were both popular. They both enjoyed parties. They were both good at sports. They liked the same kind of pizza.

"This is terrific." Sam laughed. "Pizza with pepperoni, double cheese, and hot-pepper flakes. My favorite."

Jessica grinned. "The only way to eat pizza."

Unlike most first dates, they never seemed to run out of things to say. They talked about their lives and their families. They talked about their favorite memories. They even talked about the worst things that had ever happened to them.

"OK, OK," Jessica said after recounting a couple of her own misadventures. "Now it's your turn. What was the most embarrassing thing that happened to you when you were little?"

Sam snapped his fingers. "That's easy," he said with a smile. "I fell off the stage during a school play."

Jessica's blue-green eyes sparkled. "You're kidding!"

"Nope. I was a reindeer. I stepped forward

to make a speech about what a foggy night it was and I practically landed in the principal's lap."

They hardly noticed when their pizza arrived.

By the end of the evening, Jessica felt as though she had known Sam for years. It was obvious that he felt the same way. Long after the table had been cleared and the bill had been paid, they were still sitting there, laughing and talking and gazing into each other's eyes.

"Uh, Jessica," said Sam, suddenly looking around. "We seem to be the only people here."

Jessica looked up. "Well, the waiters are still here."

Sam laughed. "I think maybe we'd better go. I don't want to bring you home late on our very first date."

Suddenly Jessica knew how Cinderella must have felt when the clock struck twelve. "Bring me home?" she asked. "You're not bringing me home unless you've got a trailer. Did you forget that I drove my car?"

He shook his head. "I didn't forget. I thought I could drive behind you—just to make sure you got back safely."

Good-looking, funny, interesting, and a gentleman, Jessica thought happily. He was perfect except for one small thing: a neon-green 125cc dirt bike. It wasn't the sort of thing she could keep from her parents forever.

Sam put his arm around her shoulders as he walked her to her car.

But she could probably keep it a secret from her parents for a while.

Elizabeth and her mother were the first to arrive at the breakfast table on Wednesday morning.

"That Jessica," Mrs. Wakefield said good-humoredly. "I knew she'd oversleep because she got home so late last night." She laughed. "Maybe Todd could think of a few tasks for her to do that would keep her in the house for a change."

"Don't talk to me about Todd's tasks," Elizabeth groaned. "Enid and I tried to buy the stuff to put up a cookbook shelf for you, but the men in the hardware store were so rude that we left without getting anything."

"I wish I could help you," her mother said, "but I doubt they'd be any nicer to me than they were to you."

"I don't suppose Dad would be much help either, would he?"

Mrs. Wakefield laughed. "You could ask him to go to the store with you. He might at least get waited on."

Elizabeth shook her head. "No. It wouldn't be right to ask Dad to go with me. Having Steven show me how to change a tire is one thing. But this would be like admitting I couldn't manage by myself."

"It's probably just as well," Mrs. Wakefield

said. "The last time your father was let loose in a lumber store they convinced him to repanel the den."

I was definitely not cut out to be a spy, April said to herself as she hurried to lunch. All this sneaking around and dodging down hallways to avoid Artie Western was beginning to make her feel crazy. He was a really nice guy and she hated to be treating him as if he had a communicable disease, but in her effort to make Michael feel more relaxed, she didn't think she should complicate things by pursuing a friendship with Artie right then. April poked her head around a corner. The hallway was clear. She began walking, then stopped. There, coming toward her from the other end of the empty corridor, was Artie Western.

"Hey, April!" he called.

April held her breath for a second, hoping that the ground would open up and swallow her. "Oh my gosh!" she exclaimed in a loud voice. "I forgot my English book!" And she raced back in the other direction.

By the time April got to the cafeteria, Michael was almost finished with his lunch. "I waited as long as I could," he said apologetically, "but I got really hungry."

"That's all right," she said, kissing him on the cheek. "You can make it up to me by taking me out tonight."

He took a bite of his apple. "Out?"

"Uh-huh. Since you didn't come bowling last night I thought that maybe we could do something together tonight instead."

"But I was going to work on the bike," Michael said.

April was just about to eat a mouthful of spaghetti, but she put down her fork. "Michael, you worked on the bike last night."

"That was my bike. I still want to check your suspension. The championship course is really rough, April. I don't want you to get in any trouble."

"I appreciate your concern," April said, "but we've still got plenty of time before the race. You can take one night off." She picked up her fork again. "There's a really interesting photo exhibit at the mall. I thought maybe we could go to that, and then get something to eat at one of the restaurants there."

"You mean you want to walk around looking at pictures?" Michael asked.

"I mean that I want to spend some time with you when your head's not in an engine."

"But what about the bike, April. There really aren't that many nights left to work on it."

April stabbed at her salad. She knew that part of the reason he didn't want to go was that he didn't know anything about photography, and he hated to be in a situation where he wasn't sure of himself. But the other part of the reason was the upcoming championship. Her one ride with Artie Western had made Michael more obsessive and determined than ever. If he thought sleeping with his bike would help him win, he would take it to bed with him every night. Suddenly April had an image of Michael carrying his dirt bike into his bedroom with him. Michael was wearing striped pajamas, and the bike was wearing matching ones and an old-fashioned nightcap on its front light. She started to laugh.

"What's so funny?" Michael asked.

"Oh, nothing." April gasped. "I just had a great idea for a photograph."

As she rinsed off the last supper plate, Jessica could feel her mother's eyes on her.

"Are you going out again tonight?" Mrs. Wakefield asked.

"What makes you think that?" Jessica asked innocently. Usually it took her hours just to get started on the dishes, but that night she had started clearing the table before everyone was done.

Her mother gave her a look. "I think it was the way you tried to take your father's dessert from him while he was still eating it."

"But Mom," Jessica protested, "you're the one who's always telling me not to waste time."

Mrs. Wakefield raised one eyebrow. "Where are you going tonight that's so important?"

Jessica shrugged. "Nowhere special, Mom."

Jessica saw a knowing look come into her

mother's eyes. "And does your date have a name?"

"Yes," said Jessica, trying to get out of the room as quickly as possible. "He has a name." She stopped in the doorway and gave her mother one of her biggest smiles. "It's Sam Woodruff." What harm could it do to tell her his name?

"And where did you meet this Sam Woodruff?" Jessica couldn't believe her own mother was interrogating her this way.

"Meet him?" repeated Jessica.

"Yes," Mrs. Wakefield said. "You have met him, haven't you?"

Jessica swallowed hard. "Yes, I met him at the Dairi Burger," she said quickly. That was not exactly a lie, she figured. There was no need to mention dirt biking.

"Oh," said Mrs. Wakefield. "Well, that's nice."

"Yes," Jessica agreed. "It is."

Six

April dreamed that she was on a date with Michael. They were at a fair, and Michael was throwing a ball at a stack of milk cans, trying to win her an enormous white bear with a pink checked ribbon around its neck. His aim was terrible. He hit the back of the booth. He hit the floor of the booth. He came very close to hitting the owner of the booth, and he even managed to hit something in the booth next door, but he couldn't hit the milk cans hard enough to knock them off. "They must be glued down or something," he exclaimed. "Really, April. They must be bolted to the shelf." April was laughing so hard that she had to hold on to him to keep herself standing. And Michael was laughing so hard that he could barely throw the balls at all. "Just once more," he kept saying. "All I need is a little practice."

April woke up smiling. The first thing she saw was the little white bear with the red bow tie that Michael had bought her when they first started going out, to remind her of the bear he hadn't won. She called it Fair Bear. That date had really happened, just as she had dreamed it. They must have been at that booth for an hour, until finally a small boy came along and won the bear and Michael gave up. It had been one of the best nights of her life. She didn't think she had ever laughed so much. She knew she had never liked a boy as much as she'd liked Michael that night.

April sat up in bed. That good-humored, fun-loving boy was still somewhere inside of Michael, and she was going to drag him out if it was the last thing she did.

When Michael arrived to take her to school, she marched down the drive and opened the door of the Trans-Am with a sense of purpose.

"Hi, April," Michael said, leaning over to give her a kiss.

"It's Friday," April announced. "*Vertigo* is playing tonight at the Plaza Theatre, and we're going to see it."

Michael imitated her high voice. "Hi, Mike," he said, "how are you?"

"It starts at eight," April said. She buckled her seatbelt.

"I'm fine," Michael continued. "And you?"

"We can stop for something to eat afterward," April said.

Michael tapped her on the shoulder. "Uh, April," he said, "I hate to interrupt, but what if I can't make it tonight? What if I have something else to do?"

"Michael Harris," she said calmly, "you've had something else to do every night this week. If you want to be my boyfriend, you'd better do something with me tonight—something that *I* want to do—or you can start dating your bike."

"Is that an ultimatum?" he asked.

"Yes," she said. "I'm giving you an ultimatum. It's that bike or me."

He shook his head slowly, his eyes on the dash. "Gee, April," he said thoughtfully, "this is a tough one. You know I love you, but there's so much more to do before the big race . . ."

"Michael!"

"And if we don't get to bed by eight every night for the next week, we're not really going to be in any shape for the championship . . ."

"That's it," April snapped. "That is absolutely it!" She started to undo her seatbelt. All those months of riding over rough terrain must have loosened his brain, she decided. And then she heard a sound she hadn't heard for some time, except in her dream. It was the sound of Michael laughing. She looked over. He was leaning against his door, laughing so hard he could barely breathe.

April started laughing, too. This was more like the boy she had fallen in love with. She leaned over and gave him a hug.

"Come on, Elizabeth," Jessica called, stopping at the back door to wait for her twin. "I'm in a hurry."

"You're waiting for *me?"* Elizabeth asked as she followed her sister outside. "What's going on?"

"Lila went out last night with the new girl, Rose, to see if she'd be interested in joining Pi Beta," Jessica said excitedly. "I've got to find out what happened before school starts."

"Oh," Elizabeth said distractedly. "Rose seems like a nice girl."

What's wrong with Elizabeth this morning? Jessica wondered. Jessica stopped a few feet from the Fiat. She shook her head sadly. "Oh, what a shame," she said in mock seriousness, "none of the tires is flat. I was really hoping I'd get a chance to see you change one."

Elizabeth climbed into the driver's seat. "Very funny, Jess."

Jessica gave her twin a look as she got in beside her. "Come on. Where's your sense of humor?"

Elizabeth shook her head. "I'm sorry, Jess. I can't get my mind off my contest with Todd."

"I was wondering what happened with that," Jessica said. "Weren't you supposed to build a boat or something next?"

Elizabeth started the engine. "I was supposed to make a shelf. Only when Enid and I went to the hardware store to get the materials, we couldn't get anyone to help us."

Jessica looked at her twin in surprise. "You're kidding. Did you ask?"

Elizabeth made a face. "Of course we asked. But the store was full of professional builders and people like that. I guess we were intimidated."

Jessica shook her head. "I can see you need some expert help. And I'm just the girl you need. Right after school we'll go over there together."

"But you don't know anything about carpentry."

"As I always say, you don't need to know how to change tires or build shelves. You just need to know something about male psychology," Jessica said.

"But Jess—"

Jessica held up her hand. "Right after school. Trust me."

Todd sat down beside Elizabeth in the cafeteria. "So," he said, snatching a carrot stick from her plate, "how's my little carpenter today?"

Elizabeth smiled. Thank goodness she'd had

that talk with Jessica this morning, so she didn't have to admit that 'his little carpenter' still hadn't bought any wood, nails, or brackets. "Just dandy," she said brightly. "I'm planning to get started on the shelf this afternoon. I should definitely have it done by the weekend." She helped herself to a french fry from his plate. "And what about my little seamstress?"

Todd looked a little sheepish. "I don't think I'm ever going to be a fashion designer," he said wryly. "The shopping I could handle, but I'm not so sure about this sewing thing."

An impish grin appeared on Elizabeth's face. "But Todd," she said in mock horror, "I've given you the most basic sewing project I could think of."

"Elizabeth, there is nothing basic about making an apron. No wonder most people just go to the store and buy them." He shook his head. "This thing has hems and ties and all sorts of things attached to it."

"But no buttons," Elizabeth said, grinning. "You should be grateful for that."

Todd speared a fry with his fork. "A man who has to sew pockets isn't going to be grateful that there aren't any buttons," he muttered.

"You better watch out," Elizabeth teased, "or next time I'll have you sew a shirt."

"I think maybe I'll just quit while I'm ahead," he said.

* * *

All the way to the hardware store, Jessica chatted about what Lila had said about Rose while Elizabeth became increasingly wary about facing the grouchy salesmen again.

"You really don't have to do this, Jess," Elizabeth said as she parked the car. "I'm sure I can find some other way of putting the shelf up."

But Jessica was already out of the car. "Don't be silly," she said, glancing at herself in her compact mirror. "Just show me where to go." She flicked back her hair.

Feeling a little doubtful, Elizabeth led the way. "Now remember," she whispered, "we want to make a shelf about two feet long to put cookbooks on. Mom says the wall is hollow, and—"

Jessica waved a piece of paper in her sister's face. "Elizabeth, please. Stop being so nervous. I've got everything written down here. There won't be any problem."

Elizabeth looked skeptical. "You don't know these salesmen," she hissed. "They're not like the boys you're used to."

Jessica stopped and turned to her twin with a concerned expression on her face. "Elizabeth," she said, "sometimes I really worry about you. Maybe you've been dating one boy for too long." She looked around till she spotted an unoccupied salesman. "Now," she said, marching off in his direction, "about that shelf."

Elizabeth noticed that Jessica had no trouble getting his attention. He stood up straight. He smiled. He couldn't help her enough. Elizabeth had to turn away so that he didn't see her smile.

"A two-foot-long shelf for cookbooks on a hollow wall," he said cheerfully. "That shouldn't be any problem at all."

Jessica leaned against the counter. "I knew you'd know exactly what I needed," she said, beaming.

The salesman had a piece of wood cut for them. He helped them select a stain and varnish. He showed them what brackets and bolts to use and how to use them. He wrote everything down and drew them a diagram. He even carried everything to the car. "Any problems," he said, handing Jessica his card, "and you ladies just give me a call."

Jessica stuck the card in the pocket of her blouse. "Don't you worry," she said, "we will." She waved as Elizabeth pulled the Fiat out of its space. "Thank you," she called. "You've been a tremendous help."

As soon as they were out of the parking lot Jessica turned to Elizabeth with an I-told-you-so smile. "There," she said happily. "Wasn't that easy?"

Elizabeth nodded. "But I feel funny about the

way we had to act to get help. We seemed so helpless."

"You still have to put the shelf up by yourself, so what's the difference?"

Elizabeth shrugged. "Well, I guess when you put it that way . . ."

"You see!" said Jessica triumphantly. "The only difference is that now you have a shelf to put up and before you didn't."

"OK," Elizabeth said. "You win. Thanks to you I can finish my shelf while Todd's still trying to figure out how to sew a pocket on his apron." The image of Todd with pins in his mouth, all tangled up in thread, made her smile.

"Only to keep things fair I might have to offer Todd my services," Jessica said with a devious grin.

"What happened to Sam?" Elizabeth teased. "I thought he was taking up most of your free time."

"Oh, Sam," Jessica's voice was bright with happiness. "He's just the most wonderful guy I've ever met."

They came to a stop at a red light and Elizabeth turned to her sister in surprise. "Is this love-'em-and-leave-'em Jessica Wakefield talking?"

Jessica flushed. "I don't know what it is about him, Liz, but I've never really felt like this about anyone before. I just feel so happy and relaxed whenever we're together. I don't think I ever feel more like myself than when I'm with Sam."

Elizabeth looked at Jessica in amazement. Several cars behind them began to honk their horns.

"Green means go," Jessica said, laughing.

Elizabeth accelerated, shaking her head. "I don't believe this. I've never heard you talk like this before."

"I told you," Jessica said. "I've never felt like this before."

"Jessica," Elizabeth said quietly, "don't you think you should tell Mom about Sam? I mean, if you're really this serious . . ."

Jessica tossed her head. "I did tell Mom about him, Liz."

"Everything?"

Jessica sighed. "Elizabeth, I'm not marrying him, you know. I don't think there's any point in getting Mom all upset over nothing." She turned on the radio. "When the time comes to tell Mom, I'll tell her," she said as music exploded through the speakers. "You don't have to worry about a thing."

April hummed as she got ready for her date with Michael. He was beginning to relax, she thought happily. Not much, maybe, but enough to be able to tease her the way he had that morning. And enough to spend precious bike-tuning time going to see a movie with her.

She smiled at herself in the mirror. Somewhere in the distance she heard the phone.

"April!" her mother called. "April! It's Michael."

April flew to the phone. "Hi!" she said.

"Listen, April," Michael said. "My dad just called and said he has to work late tonight, so I'm going to have to stay home and babysit for my sister."

"You mean you're not coming to the film with me?" April asked in disbelief.

Michael groaned softly. "I can't, April. I really want to, but I've got to stay with Janey."

He was weaseling out of another date with her, she thought angrily. He hadn't been able to come up with an excuse that morning, but now he had had enough time to come up with a great one. "What about your mother?" snapped April. "Why can't she look after her?"

"Because my mother's still in Texas, April. You know that." He paused. "Look, I'm really, really sorry. I swear I'll make it up to you."

She scowled at the telephone. Michael was probably relieved that he didn't have to go to the movies with her, she figured. He would much rather stay home and polish his dirt bike. He'd probably make his little sister watch him. What a fool she had been to think that he was coming around. How could she have believed that he really cared about her? All he cared about was dirt bike racing. If she weren't into the sport herself, he wouldn't give her the time of day.

"Hey, I know what," he said. "Why don't you come over here? We could order a pizza or something."

Oh, sure, she thought. They could order a pizza and then she and Janey both could watch him polish his spokes. "Don't do me any favors," she almost shouted. "I'll go to the movies by myself, and you can share your pizza with your bike!"

April bought herself a soda and found a seat at the front of the movie theater. She had been crying on and off since she hung up on Michael, but she was determined not to let him spoil this movie for her.

Just as the lights went down, April could make out a familiar male figure settling into the seat next to hers. For one wild moment she thought it was Michael. She turned to him with a big smile.

"We've got to stop meeting like this," he joked.

It was Artie. April tried to hide her disappointment.

Artie leaned toward her. "I was hoping you might be here," he whispered as the movie began.

And I was hoping Michael would be here, April

said to herself. But to Artie she whispered, "Me, too."

As angry as she was at Michael, when Artie asked her to go get something to eat after the movie her first reaction was to say no, out of loyalty.

"I promised my mother I'd be home early," she fibbed, not meeting his eyes.

"Look," he said gently, "I know you've been avoiding me all week, and I'm pretty sure I know why."

"I haven't been avoiding you," April mumbled, "it's just that I've been pretty busy."

"April, please," he said with a slight laugh. "It's because of Mike, isn't it?" he asked her seriously.

April made a face. "Let's just say he isn't your biggest fan."

"Well, come with me and I'll tell you why," Artie said. "I don't want you to run in the other direction every time you see me coming."

They went to a hamburger place a few miles outside of Sweet Valley, where there was little chance that they would run into anyone they knew from school. As they drove, April explained to Artie a little more about Michael, and why she had spent the week avoiding him. Artie listened in amazed silence.

"To tell you the truth, I knew he was angry with me, but I don't think I realized just how much or I would never have put you in the middle of it," he said when she was finished.

"You didn't put me in the middle," said April unhappily. "Michael did that."

They settled themselves at a table in the back. "I guess it's my turn now. Do you want the long version or the short version?" Artie asked.

"What's the difference?" asked April, returning his smile. Just being able to talk about Michael had begun to make her feel better.

Artie shrugged. "About two hours, I guess. In the short version, Mike and I are best friends from kindergarten on. We get interested in dirt biking together. We have a fight, and then we never speak to each other again." He made a sweeping gesture with his hands. "That's it, two seconds, without commercials."

"And the long version?"

He smiled. "If you want the long version, I suggest we order a pot of coffee."

They ate their hamburgers, and April listened raptly while Artie told her what had happened.

"There had always been this friendly rivalry between us," Artie explained. "You know, like brothers." He made a face. "At least I always thought it was friendly. Only as we got older, it got less and less friendly."

That sounds like Michael, April thought to herself.

But Artie seemed to have read her thoughts. "It was both of our faults," he said quickly. "By the time we got into high school, I was pretty full of myself, and I'm sure I rubbed Mike the wrong way. He was having some trouble with his father, and he had to work after school to save for his bike, while mine was given to me. Anyway, let's just say that he wasn't having an easy time." He laughed. "I had a big head and he had a chip on his shoulder.

"Eventually everything between us became personal. If we disagreed about something, Michael took it as a criticism or a putdown. For a while it was OK with the dirt biking because we were both so into it," Artie explained. "But then we started having different ideas on how things should be done, and that was it. We were on the same team, but we were working against each other." Artie paused. "And then we both fell for the same girl. She didn't ride herself, but she came to a lot of the rallies. We started trying to outdo each other to impress her." He shook his head. "It was completely crazy. It was like something out of a movie. If I did a wheelie, he did two wheelies. If he jumped six feet, I'd jump ten."

"So what happened?" April asked.

"We had a big fight about something stupid and challenged each other to a race."

"A race?" April leaned forward on her elbows. "Where?"

"You know that really rough course that cuts past Secca Lake?"

April nodded.

"That's the one we took. We were coming down this very steep incline just about neck and neck. I'm not really sure what happened, but I remember I swerved suddenly to miss this hole on my line, and Mike pulled to the right to get out of my way." Artie's voice had become very slow and quiet. "But he lost control. He went down that slope like a rock in an avalanche. Only I didn't see it, of course, because I was too busy winning."

"Oh my gosh," April gasped. "Was he badly hurt?"

"Not as badly as he could have been. Fortunately, he was wearing all his gear, so he was well protected." He took a deep breath and looked at April. "That was the last day we ever spoke to each other."

"But why?" April asked. "An accident's an accident."

"That's just it," Artie said. "Michael doesn't think it was an accident. He thinks I deliberately sabotaged him so I'd win."

April shook her head. "But didn't you explain?"

"He wouldn't let me explain. I tried to see him in the hospital, I tried to call him at home. And in the end, I got mad. We'd been best friends for as long as I could remember, but he thought I would deliberately risk his life! So I told him I didn't care if I ever spoke to him again, and that as far as I was concerned the best man had won that race—and that the best man would continue to win any race we ran together."

April sat back against her chair. "And the girl?" she asked in a whisper.

Artie laughed. "She was coming to the races to watch her boyfriend. I don't even think she ever knew either of us existed."

Seven

"Oh, no," April said as they pulled up to her house.

"What's wrong?" Artie asked.

"Look," April whispered. There, sitting in the wicker chair on the Dawsons' front porch, holding a bunch of flowers on his lap, was Michael. He looked as though he had been there for some time.

"Don't worry," Artie said quickly. "I'll explain everything."

If the whole thing hadn't been so awful, April might have laughed. *He'll explain everything. To whom?* It had taken Michael about five hundredths of a second to recognize the car and who was in it. He jumped to his feet so quickly that the bouquet fell to the ground and scattered in all directions. He ran down the walk toward them, shouting.

"What's going on? Is this what happens the minute I turn my back?"

Before April could move, he had yanked open the car door. "I can't believe this!" he roared. "What an idiot I am, sitting around waiting to apologize to you, and you're out having a good time with *him!*"

April stepped out of the car. "Michael," she said, somehow managing to stay calm, "if you'll just let me explain—"

"Explain!" Michael yelled. "Explain what? That I spent the night feeling miserable because I couldn't be with you, while you're going out with my worst enemy?"

Porch lights were beginning to go on up and down the block.

By now Artie was out of the car and had raced around to where April stood. "Look, Mike," Artie said, standing between Michael and April, "it's not what you think."

Michael pushed him out of the way. "Don't tell me what I think. You don't know anything about me!"

April grabbed Michael's arm. "Michael," she said, her voice still calm but urgent, "you've got to stop yelling or my father will be out here in a minute."

But Michael wasn't listening to her. "Can't you see he's just using you to get back at me?"

92

he yelled at April. "Do you think this guy cares about anyone but himself?"

Artie pushed his way between them again. "Speak for yourself, Michael," Artie shouted. "If there's anyone here who's self-obsessed, it's you! If you ask me, April's too good for you. Way too good for you."

"Artie, please!" April had to shout to be heard above them. "Michael, why don't you come inside with me—"

"Nobody asked you!" Michael yelled at Artie. "April and I were doing just fine till you came along." He took a step forward, grabbing Artie by his jacket. "What is it, Western? Have you dedicated your life to ruining mine?"

"Michael!" she shouted. "Artie! Stop it!" But neither boy was paying any attention to her. They were glaring at each other, their fists clenched. April didn't know what to do. She looked around, but although lights had come on in several houses, there was no one else on the street. She needed a miracle.

"Don't you think you're getting a little carried away, as usual?" Artie sneered.

Michael took another step toward him. "The only thing I'd like to see carried away from here is you!"

And then the miracle appeared. Short and balding, it took the form of Mr. Dawson, April's father, in his old plaid robe, waving a broom in the air. "I'm counting to ten," he shouted, "and then I'm calling the police. You hear me? One . . . two . . ."

Both boys froze. They turned to look at Mr. Dawson and his broom, and then they turned back to each other. "I'll tell you what," said Michael. "You're such a big man, why don't you race me and prove just how big you really are?"

"Don't do it!" April hissed.

Artie shook his head. "April's right, Michael. Look what happened the last time."

"What's the matter, Artie?" Michael taunted him. "You're afraid to race me because you know I'll beat you. Unless, of course, you cheat."

"Five . . . six . . ." boomed Mr. Dawson.

Artie pointed a finger at Michael's chest. "All right, you're on. Tomorrow afternoon, two o'clock, at the lake."

Michael stepped back. "Make sure you're there."

"I wouldn't miss this for the world," Artie said.

On a typical Saturday morning at the Wakefields', Elizabeth was usually up early and Jessica was usually sound asleep with the covers over her head and the curtains closed.

Elizabeth decided that this Saturday morning was not typical.

As she and Enid were sitting at the kitchen table, taking a break from shelf building, Jessica passed them and disappeared down the basement steps.

Mr. Wakefield looked up from the stove, where he was scrambling eggs. "Was that Jessica?" he asked in astonishment.

"That's right, Dad," Elizabeth said with a smile.

"But it's Saturday morning," protested Mr. Wakefield. "Why isn't she still in bed?"

"She's doing the wash," Elizabeth explained.

"How unusual," commented Mr. Wakefield.

Mrs. Wakefield came into the kitchen. "I wouldn't get too worried," she answered. "I think she has a date this afternoon and she needs a clean outfit."

"But she's doing our laundry, too?"

"Yes, she's doing our laundry, too." Mrs. Wakefield laughed. "It's this boy she met at the Dairi Burger. I don't think I've ever seen Jessica so happy or so down-to-earth. He seems to be a good influence." She turned to Elizabeth. "Don't you think so?"

The last thing Elizabeth wanted to talk about with her mother was Sam Woodruff. "Well, Jessica's doing the laundry," she said lightly. "I guess he must be a good influence."

Mr. Wakefield placed the frying pan on the table. "He won't last," he said gloomily. "These boys never do. You barely have time to learn their names, and then they're gone."

"I wouldn't be too sure about that," Mrs. Wakefield said. "I think this one might be different. What do you think, Elizabeth?"

"Oh, look at the time," Elizabeth said suddenly. She pushed back her chair. "We'd better go see if the shelf's dry yet, Enid."

Enid, just about to bite into a doughnut, looked up in surprise. "Now?" she asked.

"Now," Elizabeth said. "We've got to get that second coat on, or we'll be here all day."

"What's wrong?" asked Enid once she and Elizabeth were out of the kitchen.

"I'm sorry, Enid, but I didn't want to get into a discussion about Jessica's boyfriend."

"You mean your parents still don't know he rides a dirt bike?"

Elizabeth nodded. "I've tried to convince Jessica she should tell them about Sam, but you know how stubborn she can be."

"Oh, yes," said Enid, biting back a smile. "I know."

Elizabeth held up the shelf. "What do you think?" she asked.

Enid took a step back, gazing at the piece of wood critically. "It looks pretty good," she decided at last. "Very professional."

Elizabeth grinned. "It would look a lot more professional hanging on the kitchen wall than it does sitting here in the driveway." Elizabeth started to apply a coat of varnish to the board.

Enid frowned. "I don't know about hanging

it in the kitchen," she said. "Maybe you should quit while you're ahead."

Elizabeth turned to look at her. "What are you talking about, Enid? A shelf isn't a shelf until it's hanging on the wall. Until then it's just a piece of wood."

"It's just that an awful lot can go wrong when you're putting up shelves," Enid said pessimistically. "Did I ever tell you what happened to my Aunt Nancy?"

"No," Elizabeth said, shaking her head. "You didn't."

Enid made a fist and slapped her open palm with it. "She drove a nail right through a hot-water pipe. You should've seen the mess."

"You can't just put a nail through a copper pipe," Elizabeth protested.

"Aunt Nancy did," Enid said. "And Winston Egbert put the lights out in his house for ten hours once, trying to attach something to a wall."

"Enid," Elizabeth said patiently, "I'll be all right. Really. I've got the blueprint of the house that shows where all the wiring and pipes are. I'll be careful."

"You can't be too careful," Enid said. "My Uncle Bob put a hole the size of a baseball in his living room wall, just hanging a picture."

"I can't stand any more of this," Elizabeth said, laughing. She picked up her library book and her toggle bolts. "Let's go to my room while this coat of varnish dries." She put her arm around her friend's shoulders. "Unless you would rather share home-improvement horror stories with my dad. He can tell you about the bookshelf that came down in the middle of the night."

Jessica loved tennis and prided herself on being an excellent player. But in Sam Woodruff, she had definitely met her match.

"That's it!" she shouted at the end of their second set, the score tied. She slammed the ball into the opposite corner. "No more Ms. Nice Person. I want to see you run around a little."

He returned the ball with a spin. "You want to see *me* run?" he laughed. "Well, I want to see *you* run."

Anyone watching would have felt dizzy as they whacked the ball back and forth and raced around the court laughing.

"I give up!" Jessica gasped at last. She collapsed in a heap by the net. "I can't keep playing. I'm laughing too much."

Sam knelt down beside her. "Me, too," he panted. "But I want you to know that making me laugh so much is a cheap trick."

"Cheap trick, nothing." Jessica grinned. "It's my way of showing mercy on you."

He shook his head. "A terrific tennis player *and* a great sense of humor," he said. He was still smiling, but a note of seriousness had come into his voice.

Jessica felt her cheeks burn. "*And* I'm a natural blonde," she said with a toss of her head.

Sam reached over and touched her hair. "You're sure this isn't a wig?" he teased, his voice soft and his eyes on hers.

The tennis court disappeared. The sounds of the traffic and the players on the other courts vanished. All Jessica could see was Sam. All she could hear was the beating of her heart. It was suddenly clear to her just how much she did like him.

And then there was a voice in her head saying, *What about Mom? What's she going to say when she finds out I've fallen for a dirt biker?* Just as Sam's lips were about to touch hers, Jessica pulled away.

"Oh my gosh," she cried, jumping to her feet. "My mother is going to be furious. I promised her I'd be home an hour ago!"

But Sam was standing beside her, his arms around her. "Hey," he whispered, "was it something I said?"

She looked into his eyes and they kissed. *Well, I did try, didn't I?* Jessica said to herself.

"OK," said Elizabeth gamely, "here goes!" She was holding her father's drill in her hands as though it were a gun.

Enid stood back away from the wall. "Frankly, those things terrify me," she said.

With a grim expression, Elizabeth faced the wall. "You're sure we've marked the holes evenly?" she asked again.

There was a sigh from behind her. "Elizabeth," Enid said patiently, "we measured it four times. It's even. You know, it's a good thing you weren't commissioned to put up the Leaning Tower of Pisa," Enid joked. "You would have changed the face of Europe single-handedly."

Despite the fact that both she and Enid kept their eyes closed through most of the drilling, Elizabeth managed to put in four neat holes. She had one bracket up and was feeling pretty pleased with herself when the telephone rang.

It was April, wanting to speak with Jessica.

"She's not here, April," Elizabeth said. "I'm not sure when she'll be back."

"You don't know where she is, do you?" April asked hopefully.

"She was going to play tennis, but I'm not sure where." Something in April's voice caught Elizabeth's attention. "Um, April," she said hesitantly, "is anything wrong? You sound a little upset."

"Oh, no, no," April said quickly, sounding even more upset. "No, everything's fine."

"Because if I could help . . ."

April held the receiver tightly. It had taken

her all morning to decide what to do about the race. For a while she had told herself that she should just leave them to it. Then she'd decided that she had to stop them, but she needed help. She needed the help of someone who understood racing, someone Michael might listen to. And that was when she had thought of Sam. Michael liked Sam and respected him. The only trouble was, Sam wasn't at home; April had hoped that he was there with Jessica Wakefield. That was why she had called the Wakefields' house. She stared at the phone, feeling helpless. Now what was she going to do?

"April?" Elizabeth said gently. "Are you sure you're all right?"

The gentle voice was all April needed. "No," she blurted out. "No, I'm not all right. I think something terrible's going to happen." As quickly as she could, she told Elizabeth about the feud between Michael and Artie, and the run-in they had had the night before.

Elizabeth glanced at her watch. "If they're supposed to race at two, we'd better hurry," she said. "There's not much time. Enid and I will pick you in five minutes."

"What's up?" Enid asked when Elizabeth hung up the phone.

Elizabeth quickly banged the second bracket into place. "This shelf, for one thing," she said. She grabbed her bag with one hand and Enid with the other. "Come on," she ordered. "I'll tell you what else on the way."

* * *

It was the perfect day for a race. The sky was clear and sunny, the ground was hard. Michael and Artie parked their bikes near the lake and discussed the course they would take.

"I say we take the same route as last time," Michael said, staring toward the horizon, where the hill dropped sharply.

Artie shook his head. "Oh, no, Mike. I'm not going that way again. It's too dangerous."

Michael turned back to him. "You owe me this, Artie. I won't take no for an answer."

"Well, you're going to have to."

"Look, I'm the one who was hurt, and I'm not afraid. So why should you be?" Michael smiled coldly. "Or are you worried you won't be able to cheat this time?"

"That does it," Artie said, turning away. "You want to take that course, we'll take it. Let's go."

Michael and Artie were just strapping on their helmets when April, Elizabeth, and Enid pulled up at the top of the ridge.

"Michael!" April called as she jumped out of the car. "Michael!"

Michael glanced over his shoulder to see who it was, then turned back as though he hadn't seen anyone. "Just give me the word," he said to Artie.

Artie nodded.

April came skidding down the slope.

"Michael!" she screamed. "Artie! Wait a minute. Please wait!" Breathless, she reached them.

"Forget it, April," Michael said without looking at her. "There's nothing you can say that will make me change my mind."

Elizabeth came up beside April. "You could at least listen," she said.

Michael pulled down his visor. "No, I couldn't."

April grabbed hold of Artie. "Please, Artie," she pleaded. "Can't you see what a stupid idea this is?"

Artie pulled down his visor. "I've got my pride, too, April," he mumbled. "I can't back out now."

"Whenever you're ready," Michael called.

"On your mark," called Artie.

"Get set," yelled Michael.

April grabbed hold of Elizabeth's hand as the engines roared into action.

April was frozen as she watched Michael and Artie fly over the rough terrain. They were almost even from the start. Then, as they reached the steep incline, Michael swerved suddenly. As Michael pulled to the right, he cut directly into Artie's path. Artie turned sharply to avoid a crash.

April screamed as Artie's bike went out of control and he pitched over the bars, somersaulting through the air like a rag doll. It was something out of her worst nightmare. Immediately she started running down the slope.

"Please, let him be all right," she whispered out loud, stumbling over the rocky incline. "Please, please, please."

April and Michael reached Artie at the same moment. "Let me look at him," Michael gasped, trying to get around her. He had thrown off his helmet and his face was pale.

April turned to him with tears in her eyes. "Haven't you done enough?" she screamed. "If you weren't so stubborn, so stupid, this never would have happened." She pushed him back. "Why don't you just get out of here?"

As she sat between April and Enid at the hospital, Elizabeth couldn't help thinking that despite the soft colors and the warm lighting, the waiting room felt cold and uncomfortable. And the silence was unbearable.

Michael was sitting by himself on the other side of the room, looking more miserable than she had ever seen anyone look. He had been the one to go for an ambulance. Now they all sat waiting for some word from the doctors. It seemed as though they had been waiting for days, but in fact it had only been a little more than an hour.

Elizabeth leaned over and touched April's hand. "Don't you think one of us should go over and ask Michael if he wants to sit with us?" she whispered. "He looks so upset."

"He should be upset," April said, glancing at the clock.

A few minutes later, Michael stood up and came over to them. He stopped in front of April, his hands in his pockets and his eyes on the floor. "April," he said softly, "I want to apologize. For everything. The way I treated Artie . . . the way I've treated you . . ."

April stared through him in stony silence.

He squatted down so that he could look into her eyes. "April," he whispered. "Please listen to me. This afternoon has made me see how wrong I was." He swallowed hard. "Accidents really do happen. I see that now."

April leaned toward him. "It's too late to say you're sorry, Michael. And it's way too late to say you were wrong. You should have patched things up with Artie months ago, but instead you blamed him for everything." She stood up so quickly that he fell over. "For your sake, Michael, I hope that Artie's OK. Because you have nobody to blame but yourself." She stepped over him and strode down the hall.

Eight

"I'll be home a little late from school today," Elizabeth announced at breakfast on Monday morning. "Todd and I are going to the hospital to visit Artie."

Jessica ducked behind the cereal box. She knew that whenever the subject of Artie's accident came up, her mother was reminded of how much she hated motorcycles.

Mrs. Wakefield looked up from the paper she was reading. "His poor parents," she said, not for the first time. "They must be so relieved that he's going to be all right." She shook her head. "I don't know what they were thinking of, riding over cliffs on motorcycles."

"Dirt bikes," Jessica muttered, her eyes on the nutritional information she was reading so intently.

But her mother wasn't interested in the differences between motorcycles and dirt bikes. "They are so dangerous," Mrs. Wakefield continued. "I think it's crazy that any parent would let their kid drive a motorcycle."

Artie's injuries had turned out to be relatively minor. He had a dislocated shoulder, a broken rib, and some bad cuts and scrapes.

Jessica gave up on the cereal box. She looked at her sister. "Actually," she said, as though Elizabeth had asked her a question, "I've heard that dirt bike racing is a very well-organized sport with a very good safety record."

Mrs. Wakefield pursed her lips. "There's nothing safe about riding down mountains."

Jessica's eyes pleaded with her sister from across the table. Elizabeth had vowed that she would not get involved, but Jessica was desperately hoping she would change her mind. *Please*, Jessica silently begged, *this isn't like all the other times you've had to bail me out. This is important. I really care about Sam.*

Just when Jessica was about to give up, Elizabeth cleared her throat. "Artie and Michael are both excellent, experienced riders," she said. "What happened Saturday was an accident. An accident can happen anywhere."

Jessica gave her sister a grateful smile.

Elizabeth smiled back.

"From what I understand, the riders are very well protected and have some very strict rules," offered Mr. Wakefield, helping himself to another glass of juice.

Mrs. Wakefield gave him a look. "All I can say is, I'm glad none of our children is foolish enough to be involved in anything like that." Instinctively she glanced over at Jessica. "Especially not after what happened to Elizabeth."

Jessica swallowed some juice the wrong way and began to cough.

"So," Elizabeth said brightly, "I've only got one more task to do and I'm done!"

"Well," said her mother, happy to change the subject, too, "I certainly am pleased with the shelf you put up."

"So what is it this time?" her father joked. "Are you going to install all new plumbing in the house?"

"Close," Elizabeth laughed. "But it's something a little more basic than that."

"How about putting a stall shower in our bathroom?" Jessica suggested.

Elizabeth rolled her eyes. "Maybe next time. Today I'm just going to change a faucet washer in our bathroom."

"It's about time," Jessica said. "Talk about water torture! That dripping is driving me crazy."

"I could give you a hand if you want," Mr. Wakefield said. "Washers have always been one of my specialties."

Mrs. Wakefield turned to him in surprise.

"Since when?" she asked with a teasing smile. "Aren't you the man who flooded—"

"Alice," Mr. Wakefield said quickly, cutting her off, "that happened years ago. Long before washers became my specialty."

Elizabeth patted her father's hand. "It's OK, Dad," she assured him. "I got a book from the library."

Elizabeth had to stop by the office of *The Oracle* after school to discuss her article for the next week's issue with Penny Ayala. By the time she and Todd arrived at the hospital, April was already there, sitting by Artie's bed, laughing over something he had just said.

April got to her feet and picked up her things as soon as they came in.

"Don't go on our account," Elizabeth said quickly.

"Oh, don't worry," April said. "I'm not going because of you. I've got to go home and do some studying." She turned back to Artie. "I'll be back for the evening visit," she promised.

Todd sat at the edge of the bed. "We just wanted to stop by to see how you were doing," he said to Artie. "Everybody at school's been asking about you."

Artie grinned. "Except that I look like a mummy with all these bandages, I'm doing just fine." He nodded after April as she vanished from the corridor. "I've got a great nurse."

Elizabeth's face became serious. "And how is she doing? She was so upset on Saturday that I was almost as worried about her as I was about you."

"I'm worried about April myself," Artie said. "She refuses to talk about the accident or Michael. She gets furious if I mention his name."

"I guess that's understandable after what happened," Todd said.

"After all, she did try to reason with him," Elizabeth added.

"She tried to reason with me, too," Artie pointed out. "And I didn't listen to her, either." He stared down at his hands in silence for a few seconds. "The thing is that even though she denies it, I'm sure she still cares about Michael." He looked up helplessly. "But she won't talk about how she really feels. I'm afraid that she's tearing herself up inside."

Elizabeth shook her head sadly. "I know what you mean. I've tried to talk to her a couple of times since the accident, but she says she's fine."

Artie made a face. "She's even furious on my behalf. She told Michael that I don't want to see him." He reached over and took a box of candy from the table by his bed, offering some to Elizabeth and Todd.

111

"It sounds like you care about Mike, too," Elizabeth said.

"Of course I do," Artie said simply. "I know it doesn't look like it at the moment," he added with a grin, indicating the hospital room and his bandaged body, "but I'm convinced he still cares about me, too."

Todd bit into a chocolate. "These are pretty great," he said appreciatively.

"You wouldn't say that if you'd been given as many boxes of them as I have." Artie gestured with his good arm. "Why do people always bring you candy when you're in the hospital when you'd really like a double cheeseburger with a large order of fries?"

"Because they're afraid of being yelled at by the nurses," Todd joked, helping himself to yet another chocolate.

Elizabeth leaned over and put the box out of his reach. "If you eat any more of these, you're going to be in here, too, getting yelled at by the nurses," Elizabeth kidded.

Artie smiled. "It's all part of my fiendish plan to get some company," he said, and laughed.

"I'm glad Artie's doing so well," Todd said as he pulled his BMW out of the hospital parking lot.

"Me, too," Elizabeth said. "Even if he is suffering in the cheeseburger department."

Todd turned into the main road. "I wish I thought Michael was doing half as well. I didn't want to say anything in front of Artie, because he's got enough problems, but I'm a little concerned."

Elizabeth looked over quickly. "What do you mean?"

"I passed Michael's house yesterday afternoon, and he was in the driveway, working on his bike."

"There's nothing unusual about that," Elizabeth said. "According to April, that's all he does."

Todd shook his head. "Yeah, I know that. But now he's really like a man possessed. I stopped to talk to him for a few minutes, and I got the feeling that his bike is the only thing holding him together."

"Did he say anything about April and Artie?" Elizabeth asked.

"At first, we talked about the big race next Saturday," Todd told her. "But once he mentioned April and Artie, he couldn't stop talking about how sorry he was and how the whole thing was his fault."

Elizabeth gazed thoughtfully through the windshield. "I know April won't accept his apology," she mused, "but Artie would. It's Artie he should be telling how sorry he is, not you."

Todd stopped the car at a light. "I wouldn't

be surprised if Artie's right, and that April made Michael feel he isn't welcome at the hospital," he said.

"You could be right." Elizabeth leaned back in her seat. "It's too bad there's no way of letting him know that he is," she said softly.

Even though Todd had managed to eat at least six of Artie's chocolates, he convinced Elizabeth he couldn't last another half-hour without a large order of french fries, so they stopped at the Dairi Burger on the way home.

"Look," Elizabeth said, pointing past the counter to where they could see the cooks grilling burgers. "If you do well with your last task, you might be able to get a job here yourself."

Todd groaned. "I wouldn't count on that, Liz. To tell you the truth, I've been having a few more problems with these little jobs than I thought I would."

Elizabeth's eyes widened. "Todd Wilkins!" she scolded him. "You told me everything was going great!"

"That's not true, Liz," he protested. "I told you I was having a little trouble with the apron." He grinned. "I just didn't mention how many times I pinned the dumb thing to my jeans. Or the trouble I had getting the sewing machine to work. Do you have any idea how *fast* those things can go?"

Elizabeth collapsed laughing in the seat across from him. "Well, since we're telling the truth, I have to admit that putting up the shelf wasn't the easiest thing I've ever done."

Todd raised one eyebrow. "Oh, really? I thought it practically put itself up."

Elizabeth helped herself to one of Todd's fries. "It wasn't the putting-up part that caused me all the trouble," Elizabeth said. She told him about fleeing from the hardware store with Enid.

"That sounds almost as bad as me in the supermarket," Todd said.

"You in the supermarket?" Elizabeth asked. "I thought you had a terrific time in the supermarket."

Todd grimaced. "Not as terrific as I may have led you to believe." He pulled in his chair. "Actually, it was a nightmare from start to finish."

Elizabeth put on her most sympathetic expression. "Poor Todd! What happened, did someone put their groceries in your shopping cart?"

But Todd was serious. "I could have handled that," he said somberly. "What I couldn't handle was being yelled at by all those people."

"Who was yelling at you?" asked Elizabeth.

"The people whose way I kept getting in," Todd explained. "I'd stop for a second to pick out a melon or take a box of spaghetti off the

"Gee," Elizabeth said, not quite managing to keep a straight face. "That does sound awful."

"And then I couldn't find the flour!" He shuddered at the memory. "I battled my way through that store for thirty minutes, looking for the flour. I'd ask one person and she'd tell me aisle two. I'd go to aisle two and it would be dog food or something. So I'd ask someone else. He'd tell me aisle six. I'd head toward aisle six and it would be salad dressings." He shook his head. "I'm telling you, Elizabeth, there were a few minutes there when I didn't think I'd ever find my way out again."

Elizabeth giggled. "I could have written an article about you for *The Oracle*," she said. "I can see the headline: 'Teenager Vanishes in Supermarket. Todd Wilkins Never Returns from Aisle Four.'"

"Very funny," Todd grumbled, but he was smiling, too. "The worst thing, though, is that my mother's mad at me now because we've already started running out of things. I didn't know that I was supposed to be looking for bargains and stuff. I just bought whatever I wanted. So now we have two chocolate cake mixes and no paper towels."

"I don't want to jump the gun or anything," Elizabeth said with a big smile, "but I'd better start thinking about what I'm going to order when you take me to Castillo San Angelo. All I have to do is replace a washer. You still have to cook me a meal." She looked thoughtful. "I think I'll have the crab salad as an appetizer . . ."

"Whoa," said Todd. "Slow down. I wouldn't count my washers before they're tightened, if I were you."

"What am I going to do, Liz?" Jessica asked, appearing at the door of Elizabeth's room. Jessica's entrances were usually loud and attention-grabbing, like the explosion of a small bomb, but on this Thursday evening she had materialized silently.

Elizabeth looked up from her homework. "You mean you're off the phone already?" she teased. She checked her watch. "Jessica, that means you and Sam were only talking for fifty-eight minutes. Aren't you feeling well?"

Jessica dropped onto the floor beside her twin. "Don't laugh," she ordered. "I don't know what's happening to me. When I'm not with Sam I'm talking to him on the telephone, and when I'm not talking to him on the telephone I'm wishing that I were."

"This sounds serious," Elizabeth said. She leaned down and put a hand to Jessica's forehead. "Just as I thought. The patient's in love."

Jessica rolled over on her stomach. "Is this what it's like?" she moaned. "It's awful. But the worst part is all this secrecy." She propped herself up on her elbows. "No wonder Romeo and Juliet killed themselves. They probably got tired of pretending to their parents they were going out for pizza with their friends when they were really going to meet each other."

"I think there must be an easier way of dealing with this problem," Elizabeth said.

"But what?"

"You know what."

Jessica looked up, horrified. "You mean tell Mom the truth?"

"Yes. You'll feel a lot better once it's all out in the open."

"But Elizabeth, you heard Mom this morning. Once she finds out that Sam's into dirt biking she probably won't let me talk to him on the phone, let alone go out with him."

Elizabeth shook her head. "You can't be sure of that, Jess," she reasoned. "Mom and Dad are always fair."

"No they're not," Jessica protested. "What about the time Mom suspended my allowance for nothing?"

"Nothing?" Elizabeth repeated. "Jessica, that nothing was a four-hundred-dollar phone bill from calling the teen party line."

Jessica waved aside her sister's objections. "OK, maybe that wasn't a good example. But there were plenty of other times."

"Jessica," Elizabeth said patiently, "I really

think you should let Mom and Dad meet Sam and make up their own minds about him."

"I'll think about it," Jessica promised.

Jessica went back to her room to consider her sister's advice. Finally she decided to call Lila.

"What do you think?" she asked Lila. "Should I tell my parents about Sam?"

"Yes and no," Lila said.

Jessica flopped back on the pile of clothes that covered most of her bed. "Yes and no?"

"Uh-huh." Jessica knew Lila was nodding her head because she could hear Lila's earrings jingling. "Yes, you should tell them you're serious about someone. But no, you shouldn't tell them about the dirt bike. Why upset them over something so trivial?"

"Well," Jessica said, "I guess that makes sense."

"Of course it makes sense," Lila said. "You know that old saying, 'Ignorance is bliss'? Well, as long as your parents are ignorant, you can be in bliss."

April decided to stop in the deli to buy herself a treat on her way home from visiting Artie in the hospital Thursday evening.

She was feeling confused. As happy as she was that Artie was doing so well, she was also miserable. *Miserable?* she asked herself as she went up to the counter. *The way I'm feeling makes miserable look happy.* In this mood, the only thing that could possibly cheer her up, even a little, was a sour dill pickle.

The cause of her misery was Michael. She was furious with him. She never wanted to speak to him again as long as she lived. Artie might be willing to forgive Michael for what he had done, but she wasn't. She had been avoiding him all week long, hoping he would get the message and leave her alone. But he hadn't. He kept calling her house. Every time she turned a corner at school, there he was, wanting to speak to her. And he looked as bad as she felt. There were dark circles under his eyes and a permanent frown on his face. He looked as though he'd lost his best friend.

And that was why April was miserable. She felt as though she had lost her best friend, too. As angry as she was, she missed him. For the past few weeks, all she had really noticed about Michael were the negative things, such as his obsessiveness and his jealousy. But now she couldn't stop remembering his positive qualities, including his sense of humor, his strength, and his fearlessness.

But how could this be? How could she wish that Michael would just disappear from her life and still miss him?

April had just ordered three sour dills when the bell over the deli door jingled as someone came in. She glanced over. Coming through the door was Michael. Her heart dropped to somewhere around her knees. He had taken a crumpled shopping list from his pocket and was staring at it forlornly.

April looked around in panic. She couldn't let him see her. The last thing she wanted was to have to talk to him when she was feeling so confused. April abandoned the counter and dodged into a far aisle. She shuffled nervously past the cookies and crackers. She had to stop feeling sorry for him, she told herself. Even if she still cared about him, that didn't change anything. It certainly didn't change the way he had treated her. He might say he was sorry, but she knew for a fact that he was still planning to compete in Saturday's championship rally. How sorry could he be if he would still do that?

April tiptoed around the snack foods. If Michael was really sorry, he would pull out of the race—especially since he was racing with one of the younger bikers, Roy, as his partner in the relay competition. Michael must know that he didn't stand a chance of winning with someone as inexperienced as Roy, she thought. But that, of course, would not stop someone like Michael. He hadn't learned anything from what had happened. He was just as obsessive and single-minded as ever. Win! Win! Win! That's all he could think of. Never mind that he had put someone who used to be his best friend in the hospital! Never mind how much he had hurt *her*!

April walked into the canned goods section, and right into Michael. He was so surprised that he just stood there, staring at her.

He was still staring at her as she ran out of the store.

Nine

On Friday afternoon Artie woke up suddenly from the nap he had been taking. Still groggy, he thought for a second that he was in the Dairi Burger. He rubbed his eyes. No, there were the pale blue walls of his hospital room, and his bed, and the dirt bike magazine he had been reading when he had fallen asleep. Artie laughed to himself. It was a good thing he was going home the next day—he was starting to have hallucinations. But then a puzzled frown appeared on his face. No wonder he had thought he was in the Dairi Burger—he could smell hamburgers and french fries!

"Artie?" asked a quiet voice somewhere to his left. "Artie, did I wake you up?"

Artie turned to see Michael standing by the door with a white Dairi Burger bag in his hands. Artie blinked. "Michael?"

Michael held up the bag. He was obviously nervous. "Elizabeth told me you were suffering from cheeseburger starvation. I wasn't sure if . . . well, anyway, I brought you some."

After all these days, Artie had been sure that Michael wouldn't come to see him, either because of what April had told him or because of his own pride. With some effort, Artie recovered from his surprise and smiled. "Are you going to give them to me, or are you just going to stand there holding them?"

"Oh, yeah, sure," Michael said quickly, hurrying over to the bed and giving the bag to Artie.

Artie started unloading the bag. He knew that coming here hadn't been easy for Michael. He was going to have to help him a little. "Three cheeseburgers? Is that it?" he asked at last.

Michael shook his head. "Uh-uh. I got you some fries and a shake, too."

This time Artie didn't hide his smile. "What, no ketchup?"

A smile flickered across Michael's lips, but immediately he became serious again. He took a deep breath and looked Artie in the eye. "And I've got an apology for you, too, if you'll accept it," he said in a rush. "April said that you didn't want to see me again. I wasn't sure I should come. But you've got to believe me, Artie; I'm really sorry for what happened." Artie started to say something, but Michael hurried on. "Not just about this," he said, gesturing toward the hospital room, "but about everything. I've been a real jerk, I can see that now. Anytime anything went wrong, or I didn't get what I wanted, I blamed you." He smiled sadly. "I don't know why I made you my enemy, Artie, I really don't."

Artie had hoped for so long that he and Michael might patch things up that now that it was happening, he was speechless. At last he found his voice again. "We were both at fault, Mike, last Saturday included."

"No," said Michael adamantly, "not this time, Artie. This time I nearly killed you and I made April hate me. How's that?" he asked. "Losing the two best friends I ever had over the same stupid thing."

Artie laughed. "Even when you're apologizing you're the most stubborn guy I've ever known. Why don't you lighten up on yourself? I'm a little battered, but you haven't lost me, Mike. I'm still here."

But Michael was too stubborn to hear that his apology had been accepted. "I don't expect you to forgive me overnight," Michael said. "But if you'll give me a chance, I want to win back your friendship." He reached over and picked up the dirt bike magazine from the bed. "And to prove that I'm serious, the first thing I'm going to do is give up all of this."

Artie could hardly believe his ears. Michael give up dirt biking? Artie leaned forward. "Michael," he said earnestly. "Listen to me, will you? You never lost my friendship. And you don't have to give up dirt biking to prove to me that you're sorry."

"Maybe that's true," Michael said softly. "But I do to prove it to April."

Artie sighed. Michael still cared about April as much as he had thought. "But what about the big race on Saturday?" he asked. "I heard you were still entered."

"I was," Michael admitted. "After the accident, I felt like I'd lost everything—April, and you. . . . I thought that if I won the championship, if I proved I could still win, then things would be OK somehow." He dropped the magazine back on the bed. "But now I realize that April was right: winning isn't the most important thing, not if it means losing the people you care about. Racing on Saturday wouldn't make things better; it would probably make them worse."

Artie had been listening carefully to everything Michael said. At last he spoke. "Winning isn't the only reason we race, Mike," he said slowly. "But for guys like us, *riding* is important. Don't you remember when we first started together? Remember what a thrill it was? How happy we were every time we got a little better? That was why we started racing—because we loved it. It didn't matter then whether we won." He shook his head. "I know I still love it, Mike, and I believe you do, too. If you really want to do something for me, then ride tomorrow for both of us."

Michael turned away for a second. When he turned back he was smiling. "You'd better eat those burgers before they get cold," he said.

"What's that I smell?" asked April, coming into Artie's hospital room and sniffing the air. "If I didn't know better, I'd say that I smelled hamburger and fries." She gave him a suspicious look. "You haven't been sneaking out to the Dairi Burger when the nurses weren't looking, have you?"

Artie laughed. "No way," he assured her. "The doctor said I can go home tomorrow. I wouldn't want to do anything to make her change her mind."

April dumped her schoolbooks on the floor and sat down at the side of the bed. "Is that why you're in such a good mood? Because you're going to be a free man tomorrow?"

"Not completely," he said, and grinned mischievously. "The cheeseburger helped a little."

April picked up a spare pillow and threatened him with it. "You're lucky you're still in bandages," she teased. "I *knew* I smelled real food. Since when has the hospital kitchen started serving burgers and fries?"

"They don't," Artie said, looking pleased with himself. "A friend of mine smuggled them in to me."

April shook her head. "You boys," she said in mock seriousness. "You can't last even a few days without a cheeseburger, can you? Who was it? Todd or Ken?"

Artie watched her as he spoke. "It was Mike," he said, hearing the excitement in his own voice.

"Michael Harris?"

Artie smiled. "Uh-huh. Elizabeth told him I was pining away for a cheeseburger, so he brought me one. Actually he brought me three. And fries, and a milkshake."

"Well, that was nice of him," April said, sitting up a little straighter in her chair. "Imagine coming all the way over here just to bring you a cheeseburger. What a guy."

Artie took her hand. "He came over here to patch things up between us, April. You know that. And I'm glad he did."

April pulled her hand away. "He waited long enough."

But Artie wouldn't be put off. He told her everything that he and Michael had talked about. "I really think we both understand ourselves and each other a lot more now than we did a year ago," he finished.

"And does he understand that he could have gotten you both killed?" April snapped. "I hope he feels awful. He deserves it."

"You're wrong, April," Artie replied. "Michael has nothing to feel guilty about. I agreed to that race with him, so the responsibility for what happened is as much mine as it is his." He cleared his throat. "And now he understands

128

that the responsibility for what happened last time was partly his as well."

April got to her feet and started angrily pacing back and forth in front of the bed. "I don't see how you can be so forgiving," she said at last. "After everything he did!"

"It's easy," he answered softly. "Michael was the best friend I ever had. I just wish you could forgive him, too."

She stopped abruptly. Her cheeks looked as though they were burning. "Did he ask you to say that?"

"Of course he didn't," Artie explained. "But he did say he really missed you, and that he can't believe he was stupid enough to lose you."

"Oh, sure," she sneered. "Michael never really cared about me at all. He just needed a good biking partner so he could beat you."

Artie shook his head. "I don't believe that, April. And I don't think you believe it, either."

"Don't be so sure," she mumbled.

He watched her face in silence for a few seconds. "You know, April, Michael told me he wanted to give up racing. He said he'd realized it just wasn't worth it if it meant losing the people he loved."

April stared at him in disbelief. "He said that?"

"He did. And I told him not to give it up. It's something he really enjoys, April. He's learned his lesson. He doesn't need to give up dirt biking to prove he's sorry. In fact, I told him to race on Saturday for both of us."

129

April struggled to fight back tears. "I just don't know, Artie," she said quietly.

"He really loves you," Artie said. "He'd do anything to prove it to you."

April nodded, looking more upset than ever.

"If we weren't identical twins, nobody would believe that we were even related," Jessica announced to her sister's back. "I mean, really, Elizabeth, *who* stays home on a Friday night to fix the sink?"

Elizabeth consulted her library book. "It's a challenge, Jess. And it's a good thing to know."

"Oh, please," Jessica said, peering at herself in the mirror over her sister's head.

"Jessica," Elizabeth sighed, "if you don't mind, it's hard for me to concentrate with you standing behind me, criticizing me the whole time."

"I'm not criticizing, Liz," Jessica said kindly. "I just don't understand why you would want to fool around with the plumbing when you could be watching a good movie or shopping or doing something else that's important." She made a face.

Elizabeth brushed a strand of hair out of her eyes and turned around. "Jess, why don't you go do one of those important things? Maybe then I could get this done."

Jessica looked exasperated. "I need to use the sink. I have a big date with Sam tonight. You may have given up your social life to become a plumber, but I haven't." She looked at her watch. "And if I don't hurry, I'm going to be late."

Mrs. Wakefield suddenly appeared in the doorway. "You've got another date tonight, Jessica? You've been out almost every night this week."

Jessica jumped at the sound of her mother's voice. There was definitely something spooky about the way her mother kept turning up when Jessica was least expecting it.

Jessica put on her most innocent smile. "But it's Friday night. I always go out on Friday night."

"Are you going out with the same boy?" she asked. "The one from the Dairi Burger?"

Elizabeth swung around so quickly that she dropped her wrench.

"Yes," Jessica said, "it's the same boy. I'm going out with Sam."

Her mother nodded. "And is Sam coming to pick you up?"

"Er . . . ah . . . um . . ." Jessica said, trying to come up with a reason Sam wasn't picking her up. "Well, no, actually, he's not."

"Why not?" Mrs. Wakefield asked.

"Because his car is in the shop," Jessica said in a burst of inspiration. "That's why. His dad is giving him a lift to the movie."

Mrs. Wakefield looked confused. "I don't get it, Jess. You've been seeing this boy almost every day for more than a week and you're always on the phone with him, but no one's ever seen him. Does he have two heads or something?"

"Of course not, Mom." Jessica laughed. "He has one very cute head. He just hasn't come by, that's all. There's no special reason."

"He's not another phony Frenchman, is he? Oh, no! Don't tell me he wants to be an undertaker," Mrs. Wakefield said, recalling some of Jessica's dating fiascos.

"Mom, there's nothing wrong with Sam," Jessica insisted. "He's practically perfect."

Mrs. Wakefield turned her attention now on Elizabeth. "Do you know anything about this boy?"

Jessica's eyes bored into her sister. *Don't mention dirt bike racing*, she pleaded silently.

Elizabeth took a deep breath. "I've never seen him, Mom," she said in a rush. "But from what I've heard he's very nice."

Jessica started toward the door. "Well, I'd love to hang around and chat with you two," she said, "but I've got to get going."

Mrs. Wakefield made no move to stop her. "He's not another rock guitarist?" Jessica heard her ask Elizabeth.

"No, Mom," Elizabeth said truthfully. "He's definitely not a rock guitarist."

"Is he older?"

"He's still in high school, if that's what.you mean."

Several minutes later Jessica could still hear her mother in the hallway, muttering to herself. "He's got one head, he's not a rock guitarist, and he's not older. Well, what on earth can be wrong with him?"

"How about a peanut-butter-and-banana taco?" Sam asked, helping himself to more hot sauce. "With chocolate chips." He slapped the table-top. "That's it," he laughed. "A peanut-butter-and-banana taco with chocolate chips has got to be the winner."

After the movie, Jessica and he had decided to stop for Mexican food. Somehow, while they were waiting for their order, they had begun this silly game of inventing the most outrageous taco combinations they could think of. And now they couldn't seem to stop playing it.

Jessica was laughing, too, but she was shaking her head. "Oh, no," she said. "You didn't say anything about dessert tacos. We're talking main-course tacos here, and nothing else. Chocolate chips and bananas put it in the sweet category."

Sam bit into his ordinary beef taco with a serious expression. "OK," he said after some consideration, "maybe you're right. Maybe there should be a separate category for desserts. How about this, though? How about a french-fry-and-bologna taco?"

"With cheese and mayonnaise?" Jessica asked excitedly.

Sam snapped his fingers "And hot sauce!" he cried. "You can't have a taco without hot sauce!"

"Mustard!" Jessica shouted. "You can't have bologna without mustard. You should know that," she giggled, reaching out and grabbing his hand. "I don't think we can allow you the bologna-and-french-fry taco, because you forgot about the mustard."

His fingers closed around hers. "OK," he said, still smiling, but his tone was suddenly serious. "How about allowing me to meet your parents instead?"

"My parents?" Jessica gently disengaged her hand and picked up another forkful of her chicken burrito. In the last few days, Sam had hinted several times that he would like to come to her home and meet her family, but she had always managed to put him off with one excuse or another.

"Yeah," he said, grinning, "your parents. You know, the couple that lives in your house and pays all the bills. Don't you think it's about time I met them?"

"Oh, sure," Jessica said, picking a piece of lettuce off her lap. "I mean, they really want to meet you, too. It's just that they're always so busy, you know. They both work and everything."

"They must come home sometime," Sam insisted. "Even the President has supper with his family and watches television once in a while."

She had to smile. What a guy! Even when he was asking her so many questions that he sounded like her mother, Sam could make her laugh. "Oh, of course they do," Jessica said quickly. "It's just that this week's been kind of hectic for them." She wiped her mouth with her napkin. "Maybe next week. I'll ask my mother, all right?"

"OK," he said, looking straight into her eyes. "I'm not trying to pressure you or anything. It's just that I really like you, Jessica." He smiled. "I was hoping that we could kind of, you know, make it official that we're going out together."

Jessica felt her heart leap. It wasn't until he had said that that she realized how much she had been waiting for this moment. She squeezed Sam's hand, barely managing not to shout out loud. There was no doubt that Sam Woodruff was the boy of her dreams. The trouble was, as long as he rode a dirt bike, there was no way her parents would let her keep seeing him. They would be too afraid that she would want to ride, too, the way Elizabeth had. Even if she swore that she would never go on his bike with him, she had the awful feeling that they wouldn't believe her. If there was one thing her parents were irrational about, it was motorcycles.

"Jessica," Sam said, giving a little tug on her hand, "are you smiling at me like that because you want to make it official, or because you don't?"

She pulled herself together. "I'm smiling like that because I've just come up with the winner," she announced. "The pineapple, eggplant, avocado, and fried-egg taco!"

"Yuck." Sam winced. "I do believe we have the most outrageous taco ever invented." He leaned across the table and gave her a kiss. "You're going to *have* to go out with me. Anybody else would think you were crazy."

April didn't realize that her mother had been tapping gently on her door for several seconds until the overhead light suddenly went on. She turned in surprise. "Oh, Mom!" she exclaimed. "You startled me."

Mrs. Dawson held up the cup she was holding. "I thought you might like some tea," she said. "You've been so quiet all evening. What have you been up to?"

"Oh, I've just been catching up on some homework," April said. "I've got a paper due on Monday."

Her mother looked at her quizzically. "In the dark?"

"I've been thinking," April said quickly. "Sometimes I like to think before I actually start to write."

"I see," said Mrs. Dawson. "Well, I won't bother you. I'll just leave this on your dresser." She put down the cup and left the room.

As soon as she had gone, April turned off the light again and returned to gazing out the window. It was a bright, starlit night with a full, white moon. April found that staring at the moon relaxed her, especially when so many thoughts were racing around in her mind. Since she had left the hospital she must have gone over her conversation with Artie about a hundred times.

She realized again how much she loved Michael and how much she missed him. Maybe Artie was right. Maybe he really had learned his lesson.

Give him a chance, she told herself. It wasn't that Michael needed to give up biking for her to forgive him. She understood how much he loved the sport because she loved it, too. It was the competitiveness, the obsessive desire to win that he had to give up, and somehow April really believed he would.

Yes, she would give him a second chance, she decided. In fact, she was going to show him that she believed in him. And she knew just how to do it.

Elizabeth was drifting off to sleep when Jessica flew into the room, switched on the light, and threw herself on the bed. "You weren't asleep, were you?" she asked as her sister slowly sat up, blinking.

"No," Elizabeth said, "not quite."

"That's good," Jessica said, bouncing with excitement. "Because I have so much to tell you!"

By the time Jessica had finished her detailed account of her date with Sam, including how much he loved hot sauce and exactly how Jessica felt when he smiled at her, Elizabeth was completely awake. "So," she said when Jessica finally stopped talking, "what have you decided to do?"

Jessica looked blank. "I'm going to go out with him, of course," she answered in amazement.

"I meant about Mom and Dad," Elizabeth explained. "Are you going to introduce him to them?"

A pained expression came over Jessica's face. "No wonder I've always played the field," she wailed. "This relationship thing is so complicated. I could probably keep Mom and Dad quiet for a little longer, but Sam won't rest until he's met them."

Elizabeth leaned forward and gave her sister a hug. "I really think having one steady boyfriend is going to be good for you."

"I'm sure it will," Jessica said. "After all, look at all it's done for you." She nodded toward the bathroom, laughing. "The faucet leaks worse than ever."

Ten

Jessica marched through the mall with the list of errands her mother had given her in her hand and a determined scowl on her face. She should never have teased Elizabeth about the dripping faucet, she thought sulkily. If she had kept her big mouth shut, Elizabeth would be out here now, instead of working on the plumbing, and she would still be home in bed where she belonged, dreaming of Sam.

Jessica put a check on her list next to "drugstore." Now all she had to do was stop by the bakery and she would be done. Jessica jammed the list in her pocket, rearranged her packages, and headed toward the bakery. Unfortunately, to get there she had to pass the Music Center. Jessica came to a stop in front of the window. There was a large display featuring a new release by Jamie Peters. Jessica hesitated for a

139

few seconds. She knew she had been spending too much money lately, and she had promised herself she wouldn't buy any new tapes for at least another week. Still, Jamie Peters was not only one of her favorite musicians; he lived in Sweet Valley, and his daughter, Andrea Slade, went to school with the twins. It seemed only right to give him some support. *But you're already in debt to Elizabeth*, a little voice whispered. *Just go in and look*, said another little voice. *You don't have to buy anything*.

By the time Jessica emerged from the music store twenty minutes later, she had bought four new tapes and a Jamie Peters T-shirt. She glanced at her watch. Somewhere at the back of her mind was the nagging thought that there was something else she was supposed to do this morning, but she couldn't remember what it was. She checked her mother's list again. The only thing she hadn't done was buy the bread and pie. Jessica shook her head and hurried to the bakery.

As soon as Jessica pulled the Fiat into the Wakefields' driveway, she remembered the other thing she was supposed to have done. She stopped the car and just sat there, a look of horror on her face. It had been important, all right.

Jessica banged her fist on the steering wheel. It was the day of the big dirt bike rally, and she had been supposed to call Sam first thing in the morning to arrange a time and place to meet.

Jessica groaned. She slowly raised her head and stared at Sam's bike sitting in her driveway. It was astounding how large and brightly colored it looked against her parents' neat garage. It couldn't have been more noticeable or looked more out of place if it had been a giraffe.

He must have decided to come get her himself. Or maybe he had called and her mother had told him to stop by. And unless her parents had gone temporarily blind in her absence, they must have noticed the enormous neon-green dirt bike in the driveway. Jessica fought back the urge to burst into tears. Any chance she had ever had of happiness had been snatched from her hands. She might as well go to Tibet after all. "Oh, what am I going to do?" she cried out loud.

Jessica was just about to start the engine and disappear into the Valley Mall for the rest of her life when she heard the door open. Her mother suddenly appeared at the top of the drive. Much to Jessica's amazement, her mother was smiling. She was standing only a foot or two from Sam's dirt bike, and still she seemed happy and calm.

"I thought I heard your car," Mrs. Wakefield said pleasantly. She motioned with her hand. "Hurry up, Jessica. Sam's been waiting nearly an hour for you. He was just about to leave for the race."

Jessica froze. Either she had gone into shock and wasn't understanding what her mother was saying, or aliens had taken over her mother's body.

"Jessica! Did you hear me? Sam's been waiting for you. If you don't hurry, you're going to miss the start of the rally."

Slowly and cautiously, Jessica climbed out of the car. "Mom? Are you all right?"

"Of course I'm all right," her mother said. "Here, why don't you let me unload the car and you can get ready to go?"

"Go?" Jessica repeated. "You mean you're going to let me go to the rally?"

"Of course we're going to let you go," she said. "You don't want to miss Sam's race, do you?"

"But Mom," Jessica said, feeling that her mother didn't understand, "Sam rides a dirt bike."

"I know that. He told us all about it, Jessica." She made a face. "Which is exactly what you should have done."

"I was going to tell you, Mom, I really was. I just—"

Mrs. Wakefield held up her hand. "Please, spare me. Your father and I are very happy that you've found such a nice, responsible boyfriend."

Jessica couldn't stop gaping at her mother. "But Mom," she protested, "Mom, you said you didn't want me to go near motorbikes."

"Well, not too near." Mrs. Wakefield smiled. "Your father and I had a long talk with Sam,

142

and he understands exactly how we feel. He's promised that he won't let you get on a bike without our permission. What a nice boy he is," she said, a big smile on her face.

"Yes," said Jessica, a warm glow of happiness spreading through her, "he's a very nice boy."

Michael got to his feet. "Well," he said with a little smile, "everything checks out OK. I guess there's nothing more I can do."

"Start it up," Artie said. "Let's hear what it sounds like."

Michael looked over at Artie. He looked a little pale from his week in the hospital, and he was still taped up, but otherwise he looked as good as new. "I'm really glad you could come today," Michael said. "It means a lot to me to have you here, even if it's only as a spectator."

"Just you wait," Artie said jokingly. "Next time I'll really give you a run for your money."

"No," Michael insisted. "I mean it. I appreciate you being here."

Artie was a little embarrassed by the seriousness in Michael's voice. "Hey, what are friends for?"

"I think I'm just beginning to understand what they're for," Michael said quietly. He looked over at the competitors lining up and took a deep breath. "I know I don't really stand a chance in this race," he continued, "but I really want to win it for you."

"You mean for *us*," Artie said. "And anyway, what do you mean, you don't stand a chance? You're one of the best riders there is."

Michael shook his head. "I would be if you were riding with me," he said grimly. "Or April," he mumbled, looking away for a second. "But you know as well as I do that it's a difficult course and Roy isn't really up to it."

"You don't know what'll happen," Artie insisted. "After all, it is a team event. If you get enough of a lead in the first half, he might still manage to come in ahead."

Michael sighed deeply. "That's what I thought. I gave Roy the second leg because it was the easier of the two. Only they had so many complaints about the course being too near private property that they've changed everything around." He sighed. "It's going to take a lot of skill to get through the last part of the course at all, never mind winning."

At that moment the call came over the loudspeaker for the relay contestants to assemble at the starting line.

Artie put a hand on Michael's shoulder. "Just do your best."

But the optimistic grin Artie had worn on his face for Michael's benefit was replaced by a worried look as soon as he was by himself. In his heart, he knew that Michael was right. There was no way he could win.

Suddenly his gloomy thoughts were interrupted by a breathless voice behind him. "Has it started yet?"

Artie turned to find himself staring into the flushed and smiling faces of Sam and Jessica. He shook his head. "They're just about to go." He stepped to one side to make room for them.

"How does it look?" Sam asked.

"They've altered the course, so it's even rougher," Artie said.

There was a sudden deafening roar of engines and a cloud of dust.

"They're off!" Sam shouted, his eyes bright with excitement. His enthusiasm was contagious.

"Look at Mike go!" Artie yelled.

"He's riding like a real pro!" Sam said. "I've never seen Mike in better form. It's too bad April's not riding with him today."

"Yeah," whispered Artie. "It's really too bad."

Michael took the lead without any trouble. Though the line he'd chosen wasn't the easiest, he was determined to ride at his best. The other racers seemed to disappear behind him in a shower of dirt. He saw Roy waiting for him as he climbed the hill to the halfway mark. Michael passed him the flag, and Roy sped away. Michael pushed up his visor and sat there for a few seconds, watching his partner's bike glinting in the sunlight. Roy jumped over a small ravine and vanished around a bend. *Well, what do you know,* he said to himself. *Maybe I've been underestimating him. That guy really can ride.*

Michael joined Artie, Sam, and Jessica in the spectators' area.

Sam gave him the thumbs-up sign. "You were great."

Artie slapped him on the back. "You really were."

But Michael's attention was on the course. "Any sign of them yet?" he asked.

"Just a little dust in the distance," Sam said.

"How was Roy looking?" Artie asked.

"You won't believe this," Michael said, "but he didn't look bad. He's a lot better than I gave him credit for."

Jessica began to jump up and down. "Look!" she screamed. "Look! Isn't that someone now?"

The boys looked to where she was pointing. Sure enough, just coming over the rise were two riders, almost side by side as they leaped over the ridge and headed down the steepest and rockiest part of the course.

"Who is it?" Artie asked, shielding his eyes from the sun with his hand. "Can you recognize the bikes?"

"The blue one's the guy from up the coast," Michael said. He squinted into the distance. "I can't quite make out the other one. Wait a minute, it's Roy!" he shouted. "That's Roy's bike! I don't believe it! Look at him maneuver!"

The audience gasped as the two bikes surged

forward, flying over a small ravine with their handlebars almost touching. The bikes were so close and the terrain so tricky that it was clear to everyone just how dangerous it was. A silence had fallen over the crowd. Michael shook his head. "I hope Roy isn't pushing himself too hard," he started to say, but the words froze on his lips. "That's not Roy!" he whispered, his face ashen. "That's April on that bike!"

"Don't be ridiculous," Artie reassured him. "April's at home."

"That's April. I know it is. Roy couldn't ride like that in a million years!" The neon-blue dirt bike was trying to cut her off. "What's he doing?" Michael shouted. "He's going to make her crash!" Artie tried to stop him, but Michael sprinted toward the finish line. "He'd better not hurt her, or I'll pull his bike apart, pin by pin," he shouted as he pushed through the spectators. "April!"

April crossed the finish line seconds before the other rider, and seconds before Michael reached her. Flushed and breathing heavily, she pulled off the helmet she had borrowed from Roy and sat there, blinking at the cheering crowd, not quite sure what was going on until she saw Michael rushing toward her.

"April!" Michael yelled. He threw his arms around her and lifted her off her bike. "April!" He was laughing, but there were tears in his eyes. "April, I've never been so glad to see anyone in my whole life."

"We won," April said as Artie came loping up.

"Yeah, we did," Michael said, putting an arm around each of them. "But I won something more important. I won back my two best friends."

The Wakefields' kitchen table was covered with a pale pink tablecloth. Two long white candles stood at its center.

"Well, I guess all's well that ends well," Elizabeth said, smiling across the table at Todd. "April and Michael are back together. Artie and Michael are friends again. Jessica and Sam are out celebrating his victory in the last race. My parents are so happy Jessica finally has a boyfriend they completely approve of that they've gone out to celebrate, too." She gestured toward the food on her plate. "And I've had a gourmet meal prepared for me by the best apron maker in Sweet Valley."

Todd watched while Elizabeth took her first forkful. "Well?" he asked eagerly. "What do you think?"

"Um," Elizabeth said, chewing slowly, "it's very . . . um . . . flavorful."

"It's my grandmother's recipe," Todd said happily. "Chicken and rice." He started to eat.

Elizabeth, still chewing, suppressed the urge to ask whether it was also his grandmother's rice. "It's got a nice sort of crunch to it," she said tactfully.

Todd frowned. "Is rice supposed to be this crunchy?"

Elizabeth looked across at him. She didn't have the heart to say anything the least bit critical. He had been fixing this supper for the last four hours while she sat in the living room listening to the crash of pans and the chorus of "Oh nos" that accompanied every step. There had been an hour or two there when she had wondered whether they would be eating the feast for breakfast. "Well," she said appreciatively, "I don't know about the rice, but the chicken's very good."

The salad, on the other hand, was a little on the wet side.

"I didn't know you were supposed to dry the lettuce after you rinsed it," Todd said. "This salad tastes like it's been drowned."

"The bread's nice," Elizabeth said.

"I got it at Caster's," Todd said gloomily. But then he brightened. "Just wait till dessert, though." He grinned. "Chocolate chip cookies. Made with my own fair hands."

A few minutes later Todd brought out the cookies.

"What's that strange flavor?" Elizabeth asked as she nibbled her cookie.

Todd shrugged. "I don't know, Liz. I followed the recipe you gave me."

Elizabeth took another bite. "I know it has chocolate chips and walnuts in it," she said, looking thoughtful. "But I don't taste the vanilla."

Todd shook his head. "No vanilla. I couldn't find vanilla, so I used peppermint."

Elizabeth put her cookie down. "Peppermint?"

"I didn't think it would make any difference," he explained.

"It is a little unusual," Elizabeth said.

"Still," Todd said hopefully, "it's not bad for a first try, is it? I'm sure I could get the hang of this if I kept it up. You were right," he said, smiling warmly at her. "It all comes down to practice in the end."

There was a sudden creaking sound. Both of them turned toward the stove just in time to see Elizabeth's shelf come crashing down from the wall.

"Yes," gasped Elizabeth as she and Todd both burst out laughing. "Yes, I guess it is."

"I'll tell you what, Elizabeth," Todd said with a grin. "When we go to Castillo San Angelo we can split the bill."

Jessica picked up the brackets that were sitting on Elizabeth's desk. "What's this?" she asked. "Don't tell me you're putting up *another* shelf. You haven't even stopped the faucet from dripping yet."

Elizabeth gave her sister a wry smile. "No,

150

I'm not putting up another shelf. The shelf I did put up came down during dinner last night."

"Well, I'm glad to hear that," said Jessica, sitting down on her sister's bed. "I thought you would be too involved in becoming a handyman to be interested in the new Pi Beta pledge."

"You mean Rose?" Elizabeth asked. "Is she going to join?"

Jessica shook her head. "She was really reluctant at first, but Lila convinced her that a Pi Beta is the thing to be at Sweet Valley High."

Elizabeth raised an eyebrow. "People have been known to live perfectly happy lives without belonging to Pi Beta," she teased.

"Not people who've just moved to town," Jessica answered seriously. "No matter how pretty or nice you are, it doesn't hurt to be a Pi Beta. Think of all the parties she might miss if she doesn't join."

"Not to mention all the shopping expeditions," Elizabeth added with a grin.

Jessica put her hands on her hips. "You can joke all you want, Elizabeth Wakefield," she said. "But you know as well as I do that Pi Beta can make you or break you at Sweet Valley High."

Rose Jameson is certain to get into Pi Beta—or is she? Find out in Sweet Valley High #81, **ROSA'S LIE**.

☐	27567-4	DOUBLE LOVE #1	$2.95
☐	27578-X	SECRETS #2	$2.99
☐	27669-7	PLAYING WITH FIRE #3	$2.99
☐	27493-7	POWER PLAY #4	$2.99
☐	27568-2	ALL NIGHT LONG #5	$2.99
☐	27741-3	DANGEROUS LOVE #6	$2.99
☐	27672-7	DEAR SISTER #7	$2.99
☐	27569-0	HEARTBREAKER #8	$2.99
☐	27878-9	RACING HEARTS #9	$2.99
☐	27668-9	WRONG KIND OF GIRL #10	$2.95
☐	27941-6	TOO GOOD TO BE TRUE #11	$2.99
☐	27755-3	WHEN LOVE DIES #12	$2.95
☐	27877-0	KIDNAPPED #13	$2.99
☐	27939-4	DECEPTIONS #14	$2.95
☐	27940-5	PROMISES #15	$3.25
☐	27431-7	RAGS TO RICHES #16	$2.95
☐	27931-9	LOVE LETTERS #17	$2.95
☐	27444-9	HEAD OVER HEELS #18	$2.95
☐	27589-5	SHOWDOWN #19	$2.95
☐	27454-6	CRASH LANDING! #20	$2.99
☐	27566-6	RUNAWAY #21	$2.99
☐	27952-1	TOO MUCH IN LOVE #22	$2.99
☐	27951-3	SAY GOODBYE #23	$2.99
☐	27492-9	MEMORIES #24	$2.99
☐	27944-0	NOWHERE TO RUN #25	$2.99
☐	27670-0	HOSTAGE #26	$2.95
☐	27885-1	LOVESTRUCK #27	$2.99
☐	28087-2	ALONE IN THE CROWD #28	$2.99

Buy them at your local bookstore or use this page to order.

Bantam Books, Dept. SVH, 2451 South Wolf Road, Des Plaines, IL 60018

Please send me the items I have checked above. I am enclosing $_____
(please add $2.50 to cover postage and handling). Send check or money
order, no cash or C.O.D.s please.

Mr/Ms _____

Address _____

City/State _____ Zip _____

SVH—3/92

Please allow four to six weeks for delivery.
Prices and availability subject to change without notice.

The most exciting story ever in Sweet Valley history

FRANCINE PASCAL'S

SWEET VALLEY Saga

THE SWEET VALLEY SAGA tells the incredible story of the lives and times of five generations of brave and beautiful young women who were Jessica and Elizabeth's ancestors. Their story is the story of America: from the danger of the pioneering days to the glamour of the roaring nineties, the sacrifice and romance of World War II to the rebelliousness of the Sixties, right up to the present-day Sweet Valley. A dazzling novel of unforgettable lives and love both lost and won, THE SWEET VALLEY SAGA is Francine Pascal's most memorable, exciting, and wonderful Sweet Valley book ever.

BANTAM

NEW YORK • TORONTO • LONDON • SYDNEY • AUCKLAND

AN 252 9/91